The wild cry of the dismayed Ulric arrested the hand of the assassin,
who, looking back, perceived the holy man, and instantly disappeared.

THE WITCHES' CLIFF;

OR, THE

FATAL GULF.

BOUT the sixteenth century, we are told by ancient legends, the people paid homage to the eve of St. John, "with candellys brenning and wold wake." At the period when this custom prevailed, the inhabitants of a village upon the Welch coast assembled for the purpose of performing the accustomed rites, and promptly arranged the necessary preparations: they sang, they danced, and the harper twanged his instrument to many a burst of spontaneous melody. The hour, however, stole upon them when Superstition summoned her votaries to the still and awful purpose of watching for the phenomenon attributed to the specific aider in necromantic influence, the fern-seed, and many others, to prepare for the more active measure of a portentous race round the church-yard at midnight, which was to develope the secrets of fate.

Many a panting and half trembling damsel stood in anxious readiness to scamper away to the distant field of action, to sow the wondrous seed which she firmly believed would conjure up the shadow of her destined spouse, swiftly to follow in the triple round, with scythe prepared to mow down the miraculous hemp, which was to prove the instantaneous produce of her mystic agriculture.

In this moment of anxious expectation, when the harp, and even female voices, were hushed by superstitious influence, all were electrified by the sudden toll of a bell, sounding most awfully from the neighbouring priory of St. Veyno, which, by its portentous one-note toll, unequivocally proclaimed that "the fyre of clene bonyes" had lost its efficacy; since evil spirits were undoubtedly not far distant, and were toiling for the destruction of devoted mortals.

The first sound of a bell, whose province was to chase every evil spirit from its district, led all eyes to turn, in wild alarm, from their anxious observations of the fern-seed, to seek through the twilight of a midsummer's night for the appalling symptoms of the loss of influence in their heretofore unerring talisman.

Telescopical invention had not at this period reached the lower classes; the villagers, therefore, were slow in discerning in the distance the nature of the alarm, given, as they supposed, by supernatural intuition by this portentous bell.

The mountain upon which they were elevated overhung St. George's Channel: a wide expanse of water, therefore, flowed beneath the lofty eminence; and, as to this expanse their searching glances were directed, they at length perceived a ship of the first magnitude, and in its wake they shortly discerned a small sailing vessel.

The fishermen, possessing more knowledge than the cottiers of the coast of maritime and military transactions, pronounced this "a foreign invasion, and which, no doubt, formed the evil-spirited visitation the holy friars of St. Veyno had providentially detected."

To arm for defensive warfare was not in the power of the villagers, had they considered such hostile measures necessary; which they did not, since the infallible bell was now at work for their protection; and, consequently they stood earnestly gazing, with assured expectation of a speedy miracle, which they firmly believed accomplished when they beheld the sudden darting of a *spicula ignita* from the sloop, shaping its destructive course to the vessel in advance.

The fire made rapid progress through the unfurled sails, and sunk into the area between the clumsy galleries of the forecastle and the stern, and before symptoms had become visible that the deed had been effectually perpetrated, the light vessel had tacked and disappeared, leaving the superstitious observers convinced, that, like the nautilus, it could sink or swim at pleasure.

Signals of distress were soon heard from the devoted vessel, and the crew on board could be distinctly seen in as wild commotion as the devouring flames; whilst all on shore who could command a boat would have instantly put to sea to aid the sufferers, had it not been for the unfortunate superstition which taught them to believe this fire to be the work of preternatural agency for the deliverance of the principality.

The fire increased and raged with violence, proclaiming such inevitable destruction that the ship's boats, being speedily launched, were filled to an overflow, and almost instantaneously foundered, when every individual, who had sought refuge in them and could not swim back to the flaming wreck, found a watery grave.

At this awful period, the fire had fallen through the hatchway, in defiance of every effort to subdue it, perpetrating its destructive mission so fearfully that none could remain below deck ; and soon th stern and galleries were thronged with the desperate crew, crying aloud for succour, which no one, alas! ventured to offer.

One boat alone remained on board, and which, being private property, had been securely fastened by a chain to a mast; and from which not even the force of despair could wrest it without its key, and that was no where to be found.

A sudden swell of sea came on, and tossed the devoted wreck convulsively. The conflagration raged with increasing violence, and darkness seemed visible around, from the fierce glare of the glazing broadside of the ship : when suddenly the flames assumed a blue liquid brilliancy, beaming far and wide a ghastly hue, which could scarcely fail to awaken, in the superstitious beholder, appalling apprehensions of supernatural agency.

By this transparent light, which now diffused its broad glare around, the distracted sufferers upon the blazing wreck became still more perceptible. Amid the burning sails and masts, hung by ropes, not yet in actual conflagration, despairing mortals, whose groans and shrieks and frantic cries for succour rent the air, and pierced the hearts of all who heard them. At this moment appeared that very boat, which no force could before disengage from its firm mooring, making from the consuming wreck, with oars which seemed plied by preternatural power, gifted with dragons' wings to waft it towards the shore.

The monastic bell now tolled still more heavily, and the Cambrians felt relief from their superstitious terrors, when a solemn chant struck their ears, proclaiming the approach of the monks from St. Veyno Priory, who now came pouring down the winding pathway from their monastery to the shore, bearing torches and crosses, and chanting, with all their energies, anthems of exorcism ; and with the daring courage of pious inspiration, making their rapid march to the nearest spot they could reach to that point of supernatural jurisdiction, which, for many a year, had filled this part of the Cambrian population with dismay.

This spot of terror was named, with reason, " The Witches' Point." It was a rocky headland which ran out considerably towards the sea, and contained within its spreading arms a fatal gulf, whence none who entered were ever heard of more. Above the Witches' Point arose the mountain of Plynlimmon, where, when peril foamed around the mariners on the deep, lights of that luminous brilliancy which awakened suspicion of their not being the composition of mortal hands constantly appeared, and lured the devoted unfortunates to destruction.

It had been observed in the moment when the light of the confla-gration had changed its hue, that, in suspicious coincidence, the trea-cherous beacons appeared upon Plynlimmon.   As all who were aware of the influence of these lights expected, the boat from the wreck, in despite of every signal, obstinately steered for the Witches' Point.   As the boat drew nearer to this new menace of destruction, the shouts, becoming almost frantic yells, reached the ear of the imperilled adven-turers, and arrested the attention of the principal of them, a young and noble looking gentleman, of surpassing attractions, who was supporting a young lady of great beauty, who, although almost exhausted by recent dire terrors, held, fondly grasped to her maternal bosom, a lovely boy in the first stage of infancy.

The stranger, although not comprehending one word which humanity now loudly sounded forth for his preservation, being uttered in the Welch language, of which he was wholly ignorant; yet construing the import by attendant circumstances, ordered his rowers to make for that spot, where the monks with their torches were assembled.   But vain, to all appearance, proved the exertions of these mariners to change their course; some preternatural influence seemed to impel them irre-sistibly to the very point they endeavoured to avoid.

The notes of the chanting monks were now suddenly suspended; but the night owl shrieked, and in every coming breeze were wafted melancholy sounds as if foreboding evil.   The rowers of the boat still evinced every appearance of determined resistance; yet some magical impulsion led them on, and vanquished every effort at counteraction. The devoted boat entered the fatal gulf beneath Plynlimmon, and the chant of the monks again broke on the stillness of the night; but their dirge was now chanted to a pitying requiem.

Strange traditions of Plynlimmon were in circulation throughout the principality.   Upon this romantic mountain a magnificent castle had in the early ages been erected by one of the princes of North Wales, which, in the reign of Richard Cœur de Lion, belonged to Sir Hugh de Lacy, Lord of the Marches, whom rumour declared " had bartered his supremacy of Plynlimmon to a horde of witches for a philter to subdue the disdain of a lady whom he wooed; and that these witches from that moment possessed power, through their occult art, to allure ship-wrecked mariners into their toils to feed the demons who performed eir spells."

The wild legend of superstition the monks of the Priory of St. Veyno had fostered by their acknowledged belief of its authenticity, to the infinite marvel of those who patronised the rather more probable tradi-tion, " of De Lacy having bartered his immaterial spirit to a fell pur-chaser, who inspired the remorseless atrocity of alluring by lights, and other devices, imperiled voyagers into the whirlpool which Plynlimmon concealed."   Many of the victims were rich merchants, on their return from foreign shores, which accounted for the wonderous wealth of that prosperous family; but of the present baron none had found cause to shelter any dire suspicion : for he never visited his Castle of Plynlimmon, and resided in England, or in Flanders ; and in each country was esteemed a good man. Whilst of his heir, Hugo, all believed that to cherish one degrading suspicion would be to defame truth and honour Hugo was young, and eminently gifted with mental and personal advantages ; and with a disposition so evidently gentle and humane that none had yet been able to detect a flaw in his composition.

Fortune, as well as Nature, had showered her favours upon Hugo de Lacy. His sovereign particularly regarded him ; well earned laurels crowded his yet juvenile brow ; his own estates, inherited from his deceased mother, were superabundant ; and he had been long an envy to his compeers through his betrothment to one of the most beautiful daughters of creation, the only child of Earl Harcourt.

CHAPTER II.

ONE of the youngest of the monks who had been called by the custom of the Priory to join the superstitions just recounted, was Ulric Pleydel, who had but recently become a member of this community ; one of those intellectual beings whose mind could not confine its powers within circumscribed bounds, and whose light of reason, like the orb of day, broke through all those clouds which tended to conceal its splendour.

Ulric had often reflected deeply upon those mystic bubbles, which, from his junior rank in the monastery, he was employed to carry out, though not permitted to act as a projector.

A firm enemy to every species of delusion, Ulric formed other opinions relative to the events connected with the destruction of the ship than those of preternatural influence ; and, with a heart as compassionate as his mind was firm, he resolved to investigate the matter as far as he was able individually, and thus discover and assist those who had been so cruelly imperilled.

The first difficulty encountered by Ulric was in procuring a fitting time for his bold enterprise ; but at length he managed to sally forth early on the morning after these events had been perpetrated, and, provided with what he conceived might be necessary for the success of his undertaking, he at low water commenced the fearful task of climbing the rocks into the mystic cave of Plynlimmon.

It was just as the sun had sent forth his first penetrating rays, that Ulric entered this gulf of terrors. He had not long traversed this difficult and perilous pass ere, by means of an iron-tipped staff, which aided him in the dangers and difficulties of his progress, he discovered the possible witchery which had impelled the devoted boat into the fatal bay; for the rocks encompassing the entrance, he perceived, were intermingled with loadstone attractors, but whether placed there by nature, chance, or mortal ingenuity, he could not pause in such a moment to investigate, and with which magnetic influence, he entertained no doubt, the boat's prow had been manufactured to co-operate. This discovery of the opinions he had previously formed, of the nature of the agency which here prevailed, being but too well founded, might have induced his penetrating no further into the secrets of the Witches' Point, had he not known, that the dangers which this fearful pass were presenting were those only he had to encounter in this intrusion; for he had delved so far into the secrets of St. Veyno's Priory as to feel assured he garb which encompassed him would protect him from hostilities, did he encounter even the very Witches themselves, to whose exploits his convent bell had lately tolled so loudly in solemn counteraction.

The rugged path of danger, which his wary observation of its course led Ulric to attempt, enabled him at length safely to skirt the foaming gulf, which he perceived was no absolute Charybdis, but a mere impetus, which propelled that which came within its vortex into a cavern harbour beneath the lofty mountain of Plynlimmon, and into which formidable port the intrepid monk made his daring way, where he discovered a regular path, which although impeded by many intricacies ultimately conducted him up to the lofty cresset, where those attractive lights, so fatal to many a helpless victim, were occasionally hoisted; and which, from the chemical preparations he beheld there, he felt assured were of mortal manufacture.

From this elevated point his acute observation soon guided him down a long descent into a subterranean arcade, lighted from above, and which terminated with a barrier of iron railing, reaching to its very roof. But Ulric would not retreat, and at length detected the ingenious pass, through this apparently inaccessible barrier. Having accomplished this almost marvellous exploit, he paused awhile to arrange some plausible excuse to offer for thus unceremoniously penetrating into Plynlimmon Castle, for into its cemetery vaults he plainly perceived he had wound his way; and whilst thus engaged in perplexing rumination, he was appalled by perceiving traces of newly-shed blood upon the very ground where he now stood musing.

The voice of compassion now urged him on at every hazard. The sanguinary track before him served as a guide upon his now unimpeded way to the castle chapel; but there he for some time lost his appalling clue, and in searching for it unclosed a door, which opened into a gloomy gothic hall of great extent, out of which, in the very moment of his intrusion, he beheld two men flitting; one in evident retreat from the other, who held an unsheathed dagger in his hand.

The wild cry of the dismayed Ulric arrested the hand of the assassin; who, looking back, perceived the holy man, and instantly disappeared;

whilst the monk rushed forward to aid him whom he expected to find a bleeding victim. Nor was he mistaken. The Monks of St. Veyno's Priory had intelligence conveyed to them, ere many hours elapsed, that the junior father of their community had rescued the young heir of Plynlimmon from the dagger of an unknown assassin ; and that he was detained by the wounded Sir Hugo, at his couch, to prove his guard, his counsellor, and leech.

Our adventurous Monk had also charge of the very babe who had been seen in its tender mother's arms the preceding night, in her flight from the burning wreck.

CHAPTER III.

At the period in which the mysterious conflagration of the vessel was effected, the Earl Harcourt, father of the betrothed of Sir Hugo, was bowed down in premature old age by the sorrows and disappointments of his life : but, to the better understanding of the tale we are about to communicate, we must lead our readers back to years anterior to the melancholy catastrophe before related, ere we proceed with the present state of Lord Harcourt, and his only surviving child, the lovely Lady Adela de Mandeville.

The ancestor of Lord Harcourt had been amongst the first peers whom William of Normandy raised to the dignity of earl ; and from that period until the battle of Bosworth-field nothing had intervened to cause the eye of suspicion to glance toward an Earl of Harcourt. But at Bosworth-field, the present peer, then in the blossom of his youth, had devoted himself, heart and prowess, like Thomas Howard, Earl of Surrey, to the cause of the reigning monarch ; and Henry VII., through misconception of the genuine motives which actuated this adherence, never forgave him ; for although he was more fortunate than Surrey, in escaping committal to the Tower, he found he had many implacable enemies, who mined in secret to turn the king's favour from him, and not in vain.

Harcourt, proud in conscious integrity, disdained excuses for conduct he felt meritorious, and no friendly incident having arisen to call forth the loyal effusions of his heart, as in the case of Surrey, Lord Harcourt withdrew from court unforgiven; and being devotedly attached to a lady of illustrious birth, and celebrated for mental and personal perfection, he wooed and won her; and resided in his own magnificent court, in the castle of Alba, or some other dwelling upon his various domains.

Alba Castle was situated upon the coast of Yorkshire; but exactly in what spot is now uncertain, all remains of its site, and the groves and forest by which it was surrounded, having been swept away by the encroachments of the sea, or destroyed by other devastations, but it is supposed to have stood not far distant from Whitby.

Time advanced, and Henry VIII. was called to the throne. Lord Harcourt promptly paid his homage to his new sovereign; but the secret enemies who had undermined him in the court of the late king, had spread their baneful influence over the mind of his successor, and Lord Harcourt was received by Henry VIII. as if he had been convicted of having aimed at the crown of England for his own brow; and so sensibly did this loyal peer feel this misconception of his principles that he remained not a day in the metropolis after his frigid reception at court; and nothing but the arbitrary call of duty would have led him back to it, in a few weeks after, to attend the ceremony of the coronation, when the magnificence his lordship displayed in compliment to his young sovereign was invidiously construed into disloyal insolence. And Lady Harcourt not attending the queen consort upon this great occasion, increased the misdemeanour of her lord. Her excuse of ill health was disbelieved; but conviction of its truth too soon arrived, in tidings of her ladyship's decease, in a few weeks after the return of her lord to Alba.

The offspring of Lord and Lady Harcourt had been four sons and one daughter; but ere the first two lovely blossoms of fair promise had expanded from infancy into childhood, their parents were bereaved of them by consumption; and in about three years after, their third son, and now their promising heir, was wrested from them and the world by a stroke of fate so cruel that the anguish it conveyed to the maternal heart laid the foundation of that ill health which at length terminated Lady Harcourt's existence; and when her surviving son had just entered his thirteenth year, and her daughter her eighth.

Lord Harcourt, devotedly attached to all ancient customs which the great charter and other causes had not overthrown, had despatched his only surviving son, at four years old, to be enrolled amongst the pages of a neighbouring prelate, to be initiated in the mysteries of learning and courtesy essential for his station; and after a lapse of six years he determined upon completing the education of his son in his own castle.

Amongst many who had been contemporary pages with Edward Lord de Mandeville, in the episcopal palace, was Hugo de Lacy; and the Baron de Lacy, who chiefly resided in Westmoreland, obtained for Hugo, through the interest of his young companion, De Mandeville, the appointment of page to Lord Harcourt.

Lady Adela was at this period receiving her education from learned professors, under the superintendence of her father, and aided by Dame Bostock.

Lord Harcourt, in the spring after the decease of his lamented wife, was called into Kent to hold a baron's court; and feeling the disadvantage the retirement of Alba must prove to the young persons under his care, took them in cavalcade to Vespasian Tower.

At this period the calends of May were attended to with great animation by all ranks; for, as Stowe informs us in his survey of London, " On May-day morning, every man would walke into the sweete mea-

dows and greene woodes, to rejoice his spirit with the beauty and savour of sweete flowers, and with the harmony of birds, praysing God in their kinde:" and we are also told by Hall, in his Chronicle, " that the sovereign, and his consort likewise, entered into the simple and healthful sports of these calends ;"—in proof of which he relates their pleasant adventure, upon the May-day morning, in the year 1515, with two hundred archers, attired as Robin Hood and his merry men.

CHAPTER IV.

SOME symptoms of the "sweating sickness," which had raged very
fatally in the metropolis the preceding year, began to make their alarming appearance in the neighbourhood of Vespasian Tower, in the
summer succeeding the May-day visit of Henry and Katharine to the
druid's grove; and which alarmed Lord Harcourt for the safety of his
children, whom he removed without delay to Alba Castle.

When Lady Adela had completed her twelfth year, Lord Harcourt
had so far vanquished his sorrow as to indulge the ardent wish of his
darling boy in the keeping hall during the festival of Christmas in all
the state of ancient baronial magnificence.

Hawking, hunting, or the amusements of the tilt-yard, occupied each
morning; and every evening dancing, &c., furnished the pastime.

So much of chivalric manner even then prevailed, that youthful
females, gifted by nature and fortune, like Lady Adela, received homage
from every man who approached her, as if to a deity.

Sir Hugo de Lacy, under the sanction of both paternal peers, wooed
Adela, and was accepted; but these parental lords, not quite approving
so immature an entrance upon the serious duties of wedded life as custom then adopted, determined that a year or two more should transpire
ere their hands should be united: but whilst Sir Hugo and his betrothed
were awaiting, in dutiful acquiescence, for this sage time to wed, a dire
event occurred, which changed Alba Castle into a house of bitter and
lasting affliction.

At the Christmas festivities just mentioned some foreign strangers
had been entertained, whom, it was conjectured, had, upon return to
their native country, told of the surpassing perfection of the youths of
Alba Castle in chivalric prowess: for, in some months after, six striplings landed at Whitby from the Netherlands, attended by a numerous
retinue, and, shortly after landing, sent a formal challenge to six youths
of Alba to tournay with them on a certain spot. At this moment Lord
Harcourt was in the metropolis, drawn thither by parliamentary duties;
and De Lacy advised the spirited and volatile heir of Alba to postpone
the acceptance of this challenge until the return of his father.

With difficulty Sir Hugo prevailed; for Lord de Mandeville's spirit
was, like an overcharged gun, ready to explode at even the reflected
beams of ignition; whilst the idea, too, of being the leader in cabinet
and field operating not a little upon his juvenile vanity, led his wishes
to an immediate acceptance of this call to combat: yet, he looked up to
Hugo as his superior in all things but rank and birth; and, therefore,
acquiesced in the prudence of postponement. But, unfortunately, some

sarcastic observations of the challengers, upon the young chicken awaiting the return of the paternal wing, to prove his shield in peril, having been repeated to De Mandeville, nothing could shackle him in the trammels of prudence one moment longer; and, with all the impetuosity which indignant feeling prompted, he despatched his herald Sir Guy de Lancy, a celebrated warrior, with a spirited summons to immediate tournay.

No official of civil authority knew of the manœuvres of these youthful combatants, who, left to their own devices, the following day was fixed upon for this fatal test of chivalric prowess. This change in measures had been effected wholly without the participation of Adela or De Lacy; and all that was left for them to do, when they became informed of the final decision, was vainly to regret it;—the former to send an immediate express to her father; and the latter to place, in the most impressive form of language, the necessity which Edward ought to feel of taking cool and steady prudence for his shield to the jousting; and secretly to promise the trembling Adela to watch, like a guardian spirit, over the safety of her beloved brother.

But fate was ruthless. On the eve of the day in which the final arrangement of the time for this tournay had been adjusted, an express arrived to summon Sir Hugo into Westmoreland, to receive the last blessing of his father, who was now pronounced on the bed of death; and in such an anxious moment he winged his way from Alba Castle.

At length the hour appointed for this anxious contest arrived, when the foreign and English youths met on Eskdale-side, to prove the supremacy in chivalric prowess of their respective countries. Six striplings, led on by Edward Lord de Mandeville, and attended by a magnificent retinue, were received with great, though not perhaps with equal, splendour by their adversaries. Through some coincidence in the fatalities which lowered upon this meeting, the change of time for this expected tournay seemed not to have been generally known; and few indeed were the spectators assembled—to the infinite mortification of the band of embryo warriors from Alba Castle. Antagonists being arranged, the contest commenced.

The adversary of Lord de Mandeville, when his visor was unclosed, appeared to all as a youth about the same age, and of congenial powers; and Edward, in the first onset of these gymnastic exploits, appeared to the spectators as fully equal, if not superior, to his competitor, in skill and strength; but when at length his opponent's visor was closed, and the final grand onset of attack commenced on horseback, the heir of Alba felt as if a mountain torrent was pouring down to overwhelm a purling rill. Valour, pride, and a keen recollection of the galling sarcasms which had led him on to immediate combat, sealed the lips of De Mandeville, who, promptly feeling he must be vanquished, set all his force in prowess to the forlorn object of resistance. The youthful spirit was too mighty for its powers of action; it burst its boundary; and in its fatal exertions the vital spark was, alas! extinguished.

In the moment this sad catastrophe was ascertained, Guy de Lancy, with the tones and gestures of a maniac, accused the opponent of his young lord of foul sorcery, which had suddenly inspired him with a giant's strength, to contend with the nerveless arm of a stripling; and, demanding instant satisfaction by single combat, threw down his gage.

The adversary of De Mandeville, after some moments of hesitation, in which his closely surrounding friends and countrymen loudly uttered their encouragement, accepted De Lancy's challenge; and then, to prove that no unfair advantage, in an unequal adversary, had been opposed to the valorous deceased, wholly uncovered his face; when the unquestionable juvenility of the victor vanquished every suspicion of unfair preponderance in physical power. Sir Guy de Lancy revoked his accusation and his challenge, and, in the keen anguish of affliction, mournfully wound his lingering way with the sorrowing band that bore with them to the castle of his ancestors the pale corse of the beauteous youth, whom they all regarded to almost idolatrous adoration; who had come forth with them but a few short hours since, as the rising sun of their pride, their hope, their future glory; and that sun was now set to them, alas! for ever!

Adela adored her brother; her affliction, consequently, was deep and lasting; but that of Lord Harcourt was sad and piteous. He beheld no visions in love's enchanting perspective to beguile him of the intensity of his woes. His pride, his boast, his fond expectations, his prop which had led him still to cling to life without a murmur, were roughly wrested from him; and he had now no hopes, and for a long long time no resignation, for Adela was not his idol boy. No hopes, for Adela would be torn from his protection to adorn the family of her husband; and his doleful journey through the vale of life was now to find its sombre way in cheerless desolation, widowed, childless, and forlorn.

It was not unnatural, that Lord St. Oswald should turn in anguish from the appearance of blooming youths in Alba Castle; their removal thence was, therefore, promptly effected: and no longer feeling pride in ancestral customs, he sent off the supernumeraries of his dependants to comfortable settlements. His wish seemed now to make his castle, like his own mind, a scene of desolation.

The absence of Sir Hugo at this period yielded something of consolation to Lord Harcourt, who felt towards this young knight a portion of that jealous irritation awakened towards Adela; for he mentally argued, "that, had not De Lacy been absent from Alba, he, as its most celebrated tilter, would have been opposed to the fell victor, and his darling boy spared the unequal contest;" for of its being unequal he felt conviction, from the flight of Sir Guy de Lancy, who would not have absconded from Alba, where his sole dependence rested, his lordship felt assured, had he not considered himself in fault for permitting such fearful odds, and dared not stand before the parent whose mortal happiness he had thus cruelly blighted.

Such being Lord Harcourt's feelings, it proved no regret to him, intelligence brought by express from Sir Ethelbert, "that, by order of his father's physician, Lord De Lacy was to try the efficacy of foreign climes immediately; that he, Hugo, was to accompany him, and without the possibility of his visiting Alba to utter his painful farewell."

Regular posts not having been established through England for many subsequent years, communication by letter was difficult, except by special messengers. Adela, consequently, seldom heard from her betrothed; and, as her father and Hugo were now almost the whole world to her, she felt grateful, that whilst separated from the one, she was permitted the society of the other—if society it might be termed, when she was admitted to Lord Hubert's presence only at meals, or during the celebration of Divine worship.

Time passed gloomily in Alba Castle since the fatal tilting in Eskdaleside, and without hearing tidings of Guy de Lancy, or of the return of Sir Hugo to England; and, for a whole tedious year, not a guest was admitted within the castle walls.

CHAPTER V.

About six years anterior to the death of Lady Harcourt, she found, in a detached garden belonging to Alba, a lovely female infant, picturesquely laid upon a bank of flowers. No investigation could penetrate the mystery attendant upon this deposit.

The countess procured for it a careful nurse, and had the poor foundling named Isabel.

From the moment in which this foundling had been discovered, the young and compassionate Adela had evinced the most tender interest for her; and after the lamented death of lady Harcourt, continued her benevolent kindness to the helpless Isabel by every possible means her youthful powers could devise. Adela had her removed from the care of her foster-mother, to the protection of the abbess of St. Mildred's monastery, the most contiguous to Alba of any conventual establishment in the neighbourhood. Lord Harcourt, not taking the trouble of investigating the propriety of the measure, contented himself with ordering " that the *protégée* of his lamented wife should be kindly treated; but never, upon any pretence, to be introduced within the walls of Alba Castle:" and this decree of exclusion his lordship had issued through apprehension of the possible future influence of her extraordinary beauty upon his darling son; but after the premature death of that beloved son the prompt removal of all juveniles, who were movable from the premises, presented an interdict to Adela's offering her petition for admitting her darling little Isabel into the castle.

The period at length drew near which had been determined upon for the union of De Lacy and Lady Adela, when a confidential letter arrived from the Baron de Lacy to Lord Harcourt, confessing that he had not been so fortunate in the choice of his second helpmate, as in his first; that the present Lady de Lacy, having a numerous progeny, who were not so nobly portioned as the sole offspring of her predecessor, had imbibed so dire a hatred to Sir Hugo, in consequence, that he, Lord de Lacy, absolutely feared to allow of the residence of the young pair in the same abode with her; and that, therefore, with the earl's good leave, he would arrange for their dwelling in Plynlimmon Castle.

As Lord Harcourt perused this letter, some chord was touched that vibrated through his heart a soft tone of paternal tenderness; and so sweet he found its harmony, that not a moment intervened ere a responding express conveyed to Lord de Lacy an earnest request for the residence of Sir Hugo and Lady Adela to be Alba Castle. From this moment something less sad, yet with no approach to cheerfulness, was visible in the aspect and manners of Lord Harcourt.

De Lacy at length arrived, for his espousals, at Alba, with all the ardour of tender unsubdued attachment, improved in personal graces and fascination of manner and conversation—as, his heart ackn ow (gd, and his accents enthusiastically proclaimed, was strikingly the case with the peerless Adela; and his conduct had been so noble towards his unamiable and vindictive step-dame, and so generous to all his brothers and sisters, in arranging for their ample provision, upon the lately expected death of his father, that the feelings of Lord Harcourt's approbation warmed so cordially, they melted all remaining unwillingness to receive him once more as an inhabitant of his castle; although every turn and movement of the blooming polished Ethelbert presented, before the heart-wrung parent, the painful apparition of the lost De Mandeville.

Everything in the form of tournament was out of the code of preparations ordered by Lord Harcourt for the celebration of his daughter's marriage; but all else, that could could not so effectively send barbed arrows through his wincing heart, his lordship anxiously devised to do honour to the nuptials. Open house was once more proclaimed; and nothing of hospitality or magnificence was omitted, in the splendid arrangements of this long expected-event.

As the marriage day drew near, Lord Harcourt betrayed some symptoms of anticipating parental suffering; for he issued positive orders " that no trump should be sounded within his hearing; that no sport should be permitted, which could lead to individual affliction;" and, above all, " that no foreigner, nor none in masks or visors, should try their skill in any species of contest upon his domain."

On the eve of the marriage day, throngs of the old retainers of this baronial establishment collected around Alba Castle, to be in readiness against its gates should once more unclose to permit their re-entrance.

Bands, also, of pedlars, and juglers, and rustics, assembled in vast numbers, expecting that something of a fair might be permitted. Booths, both for merchandise and exhibitions of various sorts, were erected, and every rosemary tree in the chattellany and its vicinity at length were despoiled of their branches, in readiness to strew in every path the fair bride was destined to walk over on the nuptial day, and likewise to deck the habits of all those who were to have the honou- of entering the marriage circle.

So great was the multitude assembled on the night preceding this long-talked-of marriage feast, that accommodations without the castle were so inefficient that Lord Harcourt, in the tone of his natural kindness to his vassals, permitted all of his former retainers, who had not forfeited his favour, to find shelter in their ancient quarters within his gates. Those who remained without, or had found accommodation in the vicinity of the castle, were on the alert by morning's dawn, to watch for the first symptons within the castle of this day's promised festivities having commenced : but ere this impatiently looked for morning had been illumined by one bright beam of the rising orb of day, or any visible sign evinced to the gazers, of the expected bustle within, the castle gates were suddenly unclosed, the drawbridge promptly lowered, and, to the amazement of the anxious observers, the bridegroom elect himself darted forth, mounted on his own fleet Arabian steed ; his habiliments those he had been seen clad in the preceding day—close mourning for his lately deceased maternal grandam ; his face as pale as the hue which had been the last seen on the visage of that grandam ; and all who were expert enough to form observations during so transient a view, pro-nounced that horror, or despair, or terror, marked his quivering counten-ance, as with frantic speed he rushed forward in flight from Alba Castle, wholly unattended.

But what were the amazement and conjectures of those without to those within the castle walls ? Some amongst the latter had arisen betimes, to get forward in the domestic business of the day ; and, lo ! they perceived the retinue of the bridegroom preparing for departure, maintaining a total and ambiguous silence upon the subject of their extraordinary proceeding ; and shortly after beheld them quit the castle in a troop with sorrow, and marvel at the orders which were thus actuating their conduct portrayed on every countenance of the retreating group, as they made their rapid and mysterious exit.

Scarcely had this strange and unexpected scene of silent mystery passed away, when surmises and rumours were whispered forth amongst the household, it being generally known, that at the identical moment in which these mute equestrians were preparing for departure, Dame Bostock sent a request to Lord Harcourt, for his granting the Lady Adela an immediate interview. Subsequently, it was observed the interview was permitted—that it was not of short continuance ; and that at length their lord was seen, in evident agitation, bearing his swooning child in his trembling arms to her own chamber ; and from thence it was known he had retreated to his own apartments, where he summoned his chaplains, and principal gentlemen of the household, and with pitiable internal conflict proclaimed "that Lady Adela's spousals with Sir Hugo were never to take place; and that, by desire of Lady Adela, he announced that all censure relative to the breach of contract was to rest upon her."

This statement was made public throughout the household; but it possessed no influential power to enforce general belief. Those were days of superstition's ascendency; and it proved more congenial to the taste of the household to gift such incomprehensible transactions with that mysterious complexion, than with the possibility of their beloved Lady Adela acting reprehensibly.

The provisions prepared for three days' open hospitality were now distributed to the disappointed multitude; and as the old retainers, who had been favoured with refuge within the castle precincts during this eventful night, poured out to join forces with the feasted throng, tales of nocturnal wonders, and surmises, which a sense of duty had restrained whilst beneath their lord's own roof, now under the canopy of heaven, were confidentially breathed from friend to friend, until echo, or some equally attentive babbler, defeated secrecy, and at length it was unreservedly discussed, "that in the confusion of the unexpected lodgment of such numbers, where there had not been sufficient sacks of chaff prepared to rest all heads upon, sleep had been banished from many, who had therefore passed the night sauntering through the cloisters belonging to the quadrangle they occupied, talking over the happy days they had formerly passed in Alba Castle; by which means they had unintentionally beheld strange lights and appalling figures flitting about various parts of the castle, but more particularly in and near the chapel;" and many of these observers scrupled not to affirm, to the infinite gratification of those who derived awful pleasure from believing such assertions, "that amongst the moving figures which had appalled them, they had positively and distinctly seen, not only their dear departed lady, and their ever-to-be-regretted beloved young lord, but the hermit of Eskdale-side, whom tradition had positively announced as having been murdered four hundred long years anterior to this period." After such various testimonies, repeated with solemn asseverations, of such impressive personages having arrived to forbid the banns, none could wonder, that, however mysterious the termination of these long-talked-of nuptials might appear, they should, in consequence, be absolutely dissevered: nor that, under the influence of horror, or despair, or terror, De Lacy should have fled from Alba Castle, to seek refuge or peace, or at least to escape present observation, in his father's formidable castle on Plynlimmon, where we still shall leave him, under the protection of the good Father Ulric.

CHAPTER VI.

ADELA did recover from her long-continued swoon, and, by her aspect, evinced to all around her, that had her restoration from insensibility never been effected, it would have proved more humane. Horror and woe could be traced through every line of her touchingly eloquent countenance, yet with them a tone of sublimated fortitude, resolute in the performance of duty, however torturing.

The venerable Father Richard demanded the confidence of the suffering Adela, that he might pour spiritual balms into her wounded mind; but even in his sacred function he could not prevail; nor could Lord Harcourt aid him, with parental influence, to overcome this contumacious silence, for the sympathising parent's irrevocable word as a true knight now tied his tongue in painful silence; for it had so happened, that, on the eve of her appointed nuptial day, he had voluntarily pro-

3

mised Adela, on the sacred bond of chivalric honour, " that the first boon she should ask him on the morrow should be faithfully granted;" and that boon was demanded at early dawn, in her mysterious interview, and was this—" that he himself would not command her to become more explicit upon matters which she was about to communicate than her anxiety for his happiness would permit her to reveal; nor allow others to attempt the development of secrets which, in mercy to others, she had bound herself to conceal."

Lady Adela had no consequent illness; she seemed to bear up to meet the torturing conflict, lest bodily ailment might unnerve her firmness, and sink her to the cowardice of yielding to entreaties or intimidation the dire secret which oppressed her.

Lord Harcourt marked, and mourned, the intensity of that agonising conflict which mysterious duties compelled his Adela to endure: and, as he trembled when he dared surmise, and became transfixed with horror at the suggestions of direful possibilities, he felt the warmest glow of gratitude spring in his bosom towards his suffering child, for sparing him pangs of mental anguish too mighty for his fortitude.

" Let us hence, my child," at length he said to Adela; " and try if other climes can breathe less wailful breezes for our peace than Britain."

With gratitude Lady Adela acceded to her father's proposition; assured that no other clime could breathe barbed arrows in every breeze which now blew on her.

Father Richard being too far advanced in years to admit of his attendance, allowed Lady Adela the opportunity of recommending Father Hubert, her classical preceptor, as travelling chaplain to her father; and this amiable and learned priest, Dame Bostock, and a suitable retinue, at length set out with Lord Harcourt and Lady Adela from Alba.

Travelling was not, in the sixteenth century, the luxurious pastime that it is at present; but the season was genial for the tedious process on horseback; and by this mode, the one then in chief use for long marches, the sorrow-stricken peer and his lovely child, with their attendants, accomplished their removal to the metropolis; where, in Lord Harcourt's princely manson in Thames-street, they were to pause awhile, to procure many requisites to yield them comforts on their travels. Lady Adela and Dame Bostock used for their conveyance to Vespasian Tower his lordship's travelling carriage, where the whole party on wing for the Continent were to make a short sojourn on their progress to the coast.

All at length being ready to start from London, Lord Harcourt and suite set out on horseback early in the evening of the celebrated May-day Eve, 1517, afterwards denominated Evil May-day; and, without any rumour having penetrated into the retirement of Harcourt House relative to the expected disturbance of public tranquillity, Lady Adela, Dame Bostock, and two gentlewomen, in the carriage, with attendants in cavalcade, were immediately to have followed his lordship; but some unexpected delays occurred to retard this arrangement a full hour.

Thames, or Thamise-street, at this period, measured its extent longitudinally from Baynard's Castle, Blackfriars, to London-bridge; and, as Harcourt House was very near its western termination, it was rather a long traverse through this then noble street to reach the only bridge the metropolis then boasted for crossing the Thames. Lady Adela, ever feeling unconquerable alarm in going over the "jeopardous and noyous" highway which was then permitted to stand as London-bridge, ordered the blinds of the carriage to be closely drawn, that she might remain unconscious when the moments of what she termed peril might be passing. She, therefore, saw nothing, until too late, of the assembling crowds of apprentices and others, who, upon the cry of "Clubs and 'prentices," were rushing from all quarters to Cosin-lane, Tower-hill, Southwark, &c., with hostile intent against the foreign merchants and artisans, inhabitants of those particular places, who, by the encouragement they had received, and their consequent insolence, had excited the jealous indignation of the citizens.

The travelling carriage, although absolutely formed by native artisans, bore external appearance of the contrary; and the moment these impetuous rioters, who were speeding their vindictive way to wreak their vengeance upon every foreign offender they might find, beheld the carriage, they pronounced it a German culprit; and simultaneously determined upon its prompt destruction; to effect which, they dragged the postillions from their horses, and at once cut off all resistance from the troop of horsemen they beheld ready to attend it, by dexterously closing the court-yard gates of Harcourt House, and erecting exterior barriers of carts and wains, which they nimbly pressed into their service, and with such firm effect as completely to form an insurmountable blockade.

The next exploit of these young enthusiasts was to fling open the doors of the offending vehicle, to the utter dismay of the alarmed females. The very moment the beautiful Adela was thus roughly exposed to public view, a very young man, in the same species of attire which identified the situation of the assembling apprentices, sprang into the doorway of the carriage, and with brandished club proclaimed his intent of protecting the lady thus uncourteously assailed, even at the hazard of his life.

The youth, with dexterity and strength beyond every expectation which could be formed from his appearance, flung off several ruffians who attempted to annoy the terrified females, or rout their champion; and the spirited and gallant manner in which he effected this soon enlisted for him a host of partisans. Ere many moments elapsed, his efforts for a hearing were crowned with success; when this brave stripling, a model of beauty in face, and evidently so in form, as far as the attire he was enveloped in did not clumsily disguise, now poured forth a burst of eloquence, to convince the assailants of the unmanliness of this attack upon females, whom they had so ungallantly deprived of their protectors; and to assure them, that if the vehicle which had thus excited their indignation were foreign, the lovely occupant of it, he could vouch, was a native plant as sweet as beautiful.

There was mingled with the young champion's eloquence an arch vivacity of eye, tone, and expression, that won upon all; and to the apprentices of each trade, surrounding the car which he thus guarded, he addressed something so wittily and humorously appropriate to their individual calling, that soon, as if by power of magic, he disarmed their mischievous intentions relative to the destruction of the carriage, or further annoyance of its fair occupant. They at length arrived safely at Harcourt House, where the advice of her gallant protector, and her own alarms, determined Lady Adela to remain all night: as none could say to what extent this rising tumult might prevail; or that, although her conveyance had escaped the serious hostility of these first assailants, but it might, in proceeding on her way through Southwark, encounter others who might not prove so harmless.

The manner in which Lady Adela had been thus providentially rescued from the hostilities of these assailants, precluded the possibility of seeking for the punishment of the offenders, lest, by so doing, vengeance might be retaliated upon her brave rescuer, whom she requested to leave his address, that her father might have the power of thanking him for the protection of his child. But compliance with this request he eluded, by saying, the safety of some friends called him another way, but that he would call at the gate on the morrow, with his anxious inquiries for her ladyship; and should Lord Harcourt then desire to see him, he should be happy in the honour of attending his lordship's commands.

The gallant youth then departed, with a multitude of apprentices, to execute the purposes they had armed to effect; and the moment they left Harcourt House, Lady Adela sent off an express to Vespasian Tower, to acquaint her father with the cause of her detention in the disturbed metropolis.

The alarmed father lost not a moment in flying back to the protection of his child; but by the time that he, with Father Hubert, arrived in town, they had the happiness to find the rioters had dispersed, and that the city was restored to order.

The gratitude of Lord Harcourt would not permit his setting out upon his journey until he should have evinced his sense of his obligation to the defender of his child; but May-day passed away, and the champion of Lady Adela did not appear. Independent of the gallant conduct of this youth in his rescue of Lady Adela, much interest was felt for him by all the Harcourt household, and a strong anxiety, impelled by curiosity, existed for his re-appearance; since, although seven years had shot up the beautiful boy into a transcendently handsome young man, every sweet, arch, and expressive turn in his fine countenance recalled, at one glance, to recognition, in this gallant protector of Lady Adela, the animated and mirthful *aide-de-camp* of Pan, in the May morning of 1510, and who had so mysteriously disappeared; and the same necromantic vanishment, many of the family began to entertain apprehensions, was again in operation, when the second and third of May passed away without his appearing, or Lord Harcourt being able to obtain any intelligence of whom he was, to what master articled, or to what trade belonging, although his lordship offered large rewards for information.

But no offer of recompense eliciting intelligence, his lordship's apprehensions were awakened, of this young champion being unfortunately amongst those committed to prison for their outrage against the foreigners; and apprehensive that his own suspected loyalty might prove injurious to the defender of his Adela, should he appear anxious to befriend him, he employed competent agents, whose solicitude could occasion no mischief to the object of their research, to visit and make inquiry at every prison where these offenders were in confinement; but all to no effect. Nor did it avail more successfully his lordship's awaiting in London for the final decree against the culprits; or his emissaries attending at Westminster Hall on the twenty-second of May, to witness the king's clemency, in pardoning the four hundred offenders who cried aloud to him for mercy; for the brave defender of Lady Adela was not amongst them.

As the royal clemency removed every apprehension of those who had borne any part in the tumult, this young champion not subsequently appearing, left no further expectation of his doing so upon the mind of Lord Harcourt; who, therefore, delayed no longer his departure for the Continent; but left instructions with his steward at Harcourt House relative to the mode in which his lordship wished to evince his gratitude, should the defender of his child ever appear during the absence of the family from England.

This tour of our travellers was very shortly attended with one fortunate consequence—that of revealing Father Hubert and Lord Harcourt's religious feelings to each other; and with joyfulness the latter now found he had a safe counsellor in whom he might confide. Father Hubert had long been a secret seceder from the Roman creed; and having been much in the society of Jerome of Prague, Luther, and other reformers, and having studied the Scriptures until they were engraven upon his heart, he was fully equal to yielding to his lordship every information that he required.

With internal peace and comfort, Lord Harcourt now proceeded on his tour through France, and some part of Germany; and, in little less than two years after he quitted home, he returned with Adela and the suite he had embarked with, to Alba, no longer shuddering at a residence in that castle; as he now could behold serenely the tomb which contained all whom he had loved most on earth—secure, that when his mortal substance should lie mouldering within its marble boundaries, his spirit would rejoin those whom in life he had adored.

The still silently sorrowing Adela found her favourite Isabel improved so conspicuously in personal loveliness and mental acquirements, that more than ever she wished for the removal of her *protégée* to the castle :

but this project Lord Harcourt peremptorily negatived ; for, although he had seen but little of her, there was something about Isabel, that, notwithstanding her apparent *naïveté*, led him to fear her. She was now arrived at an age to make observations upon all that might transpire upon the subject of religion, and all which, he doubted not, would be whispered in the ears of her friends in St. Mildred's monastery ; and so much presentiment of evil to his family, arising from the ingratitude of this foundling, disturbed his lordship's mind, notwithstanding every effort he made to subdue a prejudice for which he could find no certain basis, that he would have sent her, with a competent provision, far from Alba, had she not been a charge committed to his care in the last moments of his tenderly lamented wife.

But matters of more importance than the anticipations of ingratitude, soon painfully occupied the mind of Lord Harcourt. To his amazement, he received friendly intimations of his secret enemies having been mining for his destruction during his absence from England, in poisoning the king's mind with representations of his being abroad upon a treasonable project relative to the De la Poles.

Not one unnecessary moment did his lordship linger, ere he proceeded to London, where, with due form, he addressed his sovereign, praying to know his accusers, and demanding a trial by his peers. But it was not for the invidious purposes of his lordship's enemies to have these reasonable requests complied with : an unsatisfactory answer was returned, neither acquitting, nor decidedly accusing him of disaffection to the reigning monarch.

For some hours after the receipt of this reply, Lord Harcourt's indignant feelings of conscious innocence led him to the determination of never more appearing at that court where his loyalty was so unwarrantably suspected ; but some moments of cooler reflection led him to believe it more judicious to go thither in conscious integrity, than, by absence, to allow of its being said he had been banished thence. Accordingly he did appear at court, and conducted himself with such dignified composure, that each unprejudiced person present pronounced his innocence ; and Wolsey whispered to the king, that he could not but suspect that calumny was at work in the case of this nobly comporting peer.

Lord Harcourt, who had, through the aid of Father Hubert, found efficacious balms for those misfortunes which he had sustained, could distil even from these an anodyne for the blow which had been aimed at his honour and loyalty ; and his irritation upon this subject evinced its manifest effect both upon his temper and his health : one amongst other sources for mental disquietude to his lordship arose about this period from the sudden death of the next lineal descendant after Lady Adela, opening the presumptive succession to the title and estates of Harcourt to a man, not only of moral infamy, but of disloyal notoriety.

" I feel no foreboding," he would say to Father Hubert, in his moments of confidential murmuring, " that my sorrowing child will again feel the influences of love; I can, therefore, never have the cruelty to urge her upon the hopeless theme of her marrage: and, unless I soon depart from this woful scene of life, to yield the king a wealthy ward, to make 'vantage for some needy court favourite, there must at length exist an Earl of Harcourt, who is in heart a traitor; and posterity will identify my imputed disaffection with his absolute disloyalty; and thus, my reverend friend, I have to expect my posthumous fame will suffer from calumny."

CHAPTER VII.

ABOUT two years and a half after the mysterious termination of the betrothment of Sir Hugo and Lady Adela, Maud, the favourite attendant of the latter, having some missions to perform for her lady, where a horse could not very conveniently take her, set out upon her pedestrianism without any companion. The kind-hearted Maud possessed so inherently the true spirit of abigailism, that she loved gossiping above all things, save her dear Lady Adela: she, therefore, loitered some ten minutes with Dame Gabble; some twenty, according to her own calculation, with Goody Sayso; and, perhaps, some thirty or forty, or it might have been fifty, with Cicely Homestall, observing Cottar Homestall and his two comely sons piling "so deftly" a woodstack: by which inadvertent prodigality of her precious minutes, poor Maud found, when she arrived at a certain brook, over which she might have readily passed ere its current had been swollen by the influx of the sea, from which the tide reached it, her passage utterly impracticable.

How was she to reach St. Mildred's in time for her mission to prove effective? was now the puzzling question: either waiting for the reflux of the tide, or to scamper home for a genet, would equally impede her arrival at the monastery ere too late; and "then poor young Miss Isabel would feel so contentless at the disappointment of her finery; and her own dear, dear young lady would be so grieved."

"Marry, if I e'er again so carelessly tarry to gossip with such chattering babblers, or spend my time gazing after comely churls, may I be nipped and bobbed into stock-fish!" poor Maud at length exclaimed, in consternation, as she tried her weight upon the branch of a tree which overhung the brook, meditating the possibility of aid that way; but at this moment her project was stayed, and her resolution utterly demolished, for a handsome young man at this moment appeared, winding by the water's margin, mounted upon a prancing palfrey.

His riding-coat of black velvet, richly embroidered, his black velvet cap, gracefully ornamented with drooping feathers, Pretty Mistress Maud instantly reclaimed the shapely leg which she had sent roaming round the tree's branch, adjusted her petticoat and kirtle in beseeming order, and herself in readiness to drop a respectful curtsey.

"Heaven's blessing be with you, my pretty damsel!" exclaimed the equestrian, smiling; "but is it contentless with life you have waxed, that to end it is your rash intention? Or haps it you are on salliance to a folkmote with the water nymphs? If so, let me not rob you of your pastime."

"In good sooth, noble sir, I am not so dareing," responded Maud: "I was on salliance to make experiment to swing athwart the rivulet, without danger of being drowned; for I have need to speed incontinently with this fardel, to a monastery foreby; and having warelessly lost my pass at low water, were I to return home for a genet to bear me over, and to wend my way back ever so quickly, I could not be time enough for this day's jubilee at St. Mildred's West."

"Spring upon this bank, and mount behind me, if you list, and mind not the lack of a pillion," said the kind-hearted traveller; "I'll guarantee your carriage without being drowned, and your safe arrival at St. Mildred's soon."

Maude with thankfulness accepted this kind offer, feeling no alarm or impropriety or danger in the measure—so much of chivalric honour and courtesy still remained; and, thanks to the wise management of Wolsey, highway robbers had so decreased, that, as Erasmus expressed it, the nation was not more free "of wild beasts than of harmful men;" and being thus devoid of apprehension, and full of gratitude for this rapid conveyance, she was not tardy in expressing her cause of obligation, "in the great disappointment it must have proved to Isabel, had she not arrived at St. Mildred's in time, with a pair of beautiful foresleeves, and some other little matters of gaudery, which had been forgotten when the other things had been sent for her appearing at the jubilee of that day."

"May I ask, who is Isabel?" demanded the stranger.

Maud, without hesitation, repeated the history of the beautiful foundling; because it yielded her a channel in which to run forth the well-merited praises of Lady Adela.

"Wot you, will this paragon of yours and *mine*, attend this day's jubilee at St. Mildred's?" exclaimed the stranger anxiously, the moment Maud had finished her concise history of Isabel: "I say *my* paragon, for I have long time felt her such."

"Gramercy, noble sir! where could you have seen my lady?" said the wondering Maud, now more that ever certain her belief was just, of having somewhere beheld this stranger and heard his voice ere now. "Where could you have seen the Lady Adela? for, since our arrival from abroad, the nuns themselves lead not a more recluse life, and are not half so confined as she has been since my lord's ill health has become so dangerous."

"Albeit, I have seen the Lady Adela," responded the stranger; "and each time I was so fortunate is bright in my memory's recollection. But now, kind damsel, if my aid has in sooth been serviceable to you, respond yours to me. Bethink you of some friendly window in your castle, where I might obtain a view of this beauty of ours; for, to let you a little more into my secrets, I have made my steed foam, in a scamper of many miles hitherward, with a hope of accomplishing even this transient gleam of happiness."

"Gramercy! But have you no knowledge of my lord, or of Father Hubert, or of any of the habitants of our castle? for Lady Adela is not a gaper out o' windows."

"Alas!" rejoined the stranger, "the higher powers have decreed no avowed approachment for me to Alba."

Maud felt amazement; and although anxious to develope more, perceiving they had arrived within view of St. Mildred's, requested permission to alight; and the moment she dismounted, she commenced her expression of grateful feeling, whilst she intently examined the stranger's countenance; but scarcely had her acknowledgments began a rapid flow from her lips, ere every feeling was arrested by surprise, and she exclaimed:—

" Gramercy! It seemeth me, I once again behold the sporting youth who chafed with envy our lord of misrule in Vespasian Wood ; and albeit diversely apparelled, our champion too of London."

And that he was indeed apparelled differently, the astonishment of Maud testified ; for now there was no appearance of apprentice-gear— no doublet of canvas, or sackcloth, or English leather—no hose of white, blue, or russet kersey ; but, fearless of detection, was he arrayed in silks and velvets suited to one of high estate. And if he were in accordance with their seeming, Maud began to fear his strange disappearances had been really the work of magic ; and at this suggestion her heart beat painfully, and she began almost to doubt if she herself yet remained in a state of visibility—and she feared to look around, lest the personage to whom she had so carelessly entrusted her safety, might be in the very performance of his awful sorcery ; but her superstitious panic decreased when she heard again the sound of her escort's melodious accents, as in tones something approaching to chagrin he said :— " I should have been better pleased had you lacked this talent of recognition, my fair damsel.   Yet, I feel assured you have no evil intention against me ; and I entreat you will not inform your peerless lady of having met me here, for I would not that the Lady Adela, and her noble sire, should think I avoided the honour bestowed on me of permission to approach their presence.   But, to my sorrow, I am fettered by the commands of those I am bound to obey, not to go thither : yet I trust a season of more promise for my happiness may soon arrive. And now, lest I should be encountered by those who might make evil of it, I must say farewell ; and I earnestly pray you to accept these marcs to purchase a few trifles, to aid your recollection of your now old acquaintance, St. Aubin."

Maud received the gift with gratitude, and purchased some trifling articles the first opportunity ; but did not prove faithful to her implied compact in all its *points ;* for the moment she returned from St. Mildred's to Alba, she informed her lady of her singular adventure ; and repeated every word which St. Aubin had uttered to her,—communications that were shortly after conveyed by Adela to her father, with the omission only of allusion to the admiration which St. Aubin had expressed relative to herself.

Lord Harcourt, scarcely making a comment upon the champion of his Adela having appeared one moment in the homely apparel of an apprentice, and in another in that of a personage of high estate, at once pronounced, and in terms proclaiming his heart was pained by the conviction, "that the authority to which St. Aubin thus reluctantly bowed, was no other than the sovereign's: and the cause—the supposed disloyalty of the lord of Alba Castle."

Through the busy trump of rumour, the political principles of the man next in succession to Lady Adela de Mandeville, should she die without issue, at length reached the royal ear ; and Henry, after mentally adding this presumptive successor's culpability to the heap accumulated by calumny upon Lord Harcourt's head, determined to turn this information to the advantage of a needy favourite, and therefore sent off, without delay, an express to Alba, to announce, "that if Lord Harcourt wished to prove his lately boasted loyalty sincere, he would prevent the possibility of his titles and estates ultimately descending to a disloyal man, by complying with the king's desire immediately, and bestowing the hand of his daughter upon Earl Fitzstephen."

Lord Fitzstephen was too near a neighbour, and too well known to Lord Harcourt, not to cause this alliance to be recoiled from in horror by this upright peer; who, without one moment's pause, replied in terms of profound respect to his sovereign, but with striking firmness, remarking, "that he knew the Lord Fitzstephen—well knew him for one of his calumniators; and that, therefore, his revenge was to be expected. Yet he would brave it, without one recreant fear; and would prepare for the scaffold, sooner than yield his consent to the sacrifice of his inestimable child to Earl Fitzstephen."

The manly, dignified reply of Lord Harcourt penetrated its way to the feelings of the king, whose small portion of the softer sensibilities were powerfully touched by the parental tenderness breathed through every line from the man who had thus heroically dared to thwart his wishes; yet, wincing from the idea of yielding altogether, he resolved, that although he might relinquish his determination relative to Lord Fitzstephen, the daughter's hand should ultimately protect the father's head.

Shortly after forming this determination, the king, on passing to the queen's apartments, encountered St. Aubin, who was pacing, with another courtier, the gallery, when his Majesty unexpectedly entered. The difficulty with which the companion of St. Aubin suppressed his before audible risibility, upon the entrance of his sovereign, was observed almost with envy, by the mirth-loving monarch, who instantly commanded participation in their merry fancies: when St. Aubin, in obedience, recounted some ludicrous anecdotes, with such comic effect, that the delighted Henry determined that his reward should be the hand of the heiress of Harcourt.

St. Aubin was transported with joy and gratitude. A new express was in consequence despatched to Alba, with a proposition for this marriage, accompanied by unequivocal threats of all that an arbitrary monarch could, and would, perform. But threats in this case were unnecessary. The first wish of Lord Harcourt's earthly projects had now become the marriage of his daughter, to prevent the possible disgrace to his line of an unworthy successor: and, as he firmly believed, a dutiful and affectionate son could scarcely fail of proving a kind if not a tender husband, this new project of his sovereign's met his unqualified approbation; whilst Lady Adela herself felt it as an absolute reprieve from misery, as, from the period her father's health had so visibly declined, she had felt conviction that she ought to accumulate fortitude for some day becoming a victim to the arbitrary power of her royal guardian; and her apprehensions thus relieved, by an object proclaimed by fame most amiable, excited too much gratitude to admit of her utterance of a negative—could negative avail where Henry VIII had issued his decree.

Maud's encounter with St. Aubin had enabled Lord Harcourt to make inquiries after the champion of Lady Adela by name, and satisfactory information upon the subject of these inquiries had reached his lordship ere the royal mandate for this May-game hero to become his son.

St. Aubin was a posthumous child, for whom, through some carelessness in the arrangements of marriage-settlements, there had been no provision secured by his father, the late Baron Darlington. His brothers and sisters were all minors at the period of his birth, and could form no contribution for his provision:—all the expenses, therefore, of his rearing had fallen upon his mother, whose jointure was very inconsiderable. But no privations were shrunk from, by this affectionate parent, that could yield advantage to her darling child; and whilst sacrificing every appendage to her state, to defray the expenses of his education, she had lived in the most complete seclusion; and at one period when she had retired to a small hamlet near Vespasian Tower, was that in which St. Aubin performed his first May-day frolic. He had discovered, through his mother's landlord being employed in the execution of the requisite preparations, the gay scenes which Lord Harcourt was arranging to exhibit for the amusement of the king and queen; and in compliance with his wild anxiety to become a spectato of them, Lady Darlington permitted him to attend in the disguise of a rustic, and she herself assumed the garb of an old cottager, for the purpose of watching over the conduct of her volatile boy whilst herding with the multitude; and soon she beheld, with dismay, the active part he spontaneously undertook in a moment of her separation from him, and with impatience she watched for an opportunity of calling him away; for it was not her wish to permit his attracting notice, until his education should have been sufficiently advanced to gift him with the power of securing approbation. But when she discovered symptoms of the fascinations of the youthful May Queen being in evident operation over the fancy of this treasure of her anxious care, terror at the consequences to be apprehended, were he to become eventually attached to the daughter of a suspected traitor, led her, without a moment's hesitation, to exert her maternal influence; and not only did she fly away with her reluctant son from the gay scenes of that morning, but from the neighbourhood altogether.

Fate, however, counteracted the manœuvring of the anxious mother; who, by practising the most rigid economy, had accomplished the education of her son with credit to herself, and to his able instructors; and at length returned with him from the University of Paris to London, full of hope, that, through the influence of her friends at court, the king might be induced to provide for him.

The friends of Lady Darlington proved sterling. They awakened a strong predisposition in the sovereign's mind to befriend the youth, and which, upon introduction, St. Aubin improved effectually by the graceful fascination of his manners; although his long-wished for introduction to the king had been effected under the inauspicious appearance of a state culprit.

Lady Darlington was establishing herself in something of a suitable residence in the village of Charing—to be thus near the metropolis, to await the golden opportunity of her son's introduction to Henry—when the volatile St. Aubin, anxious to see the pastimes of the morrow, took French leave of his mother, proceeded to Westminster on foot, on the evening of the 30th of April, 1517, and then proceeded in a boat to Tower Hill, where his foster-brother was apprenticed to a goldsmith, to inquire from him, if any of the city parishes were to unite on the morrow, to bring in May-poles, that he might attend the procession as a spectator: and scarcely had he arrived on Tower Hill, when the tumult called his foster-brother and fellow-apprentices to prepare for joining the insurgents. The foster-mother of St. Aubin had lately formed a second marriage, and it was with a foreigner. Affection to the tender nurse of his infancy led him instantaneously to sally to her residence, and to aid in her defence; and, in the Sunday suit of his foster-brother, promptly assumed, enter the city, that, as a London 'prentice, he might be able to effect more for the preservation of his nurse's property and personal safety, than as a stranger. He sallied forth, accompanied by the young goldsmith; and on his way to the place of his destination, he was unexpectedly called to the protection of her whose youthful image still retained the first place in his admiration.

The juvenile pride of St. Aubin revolted from acknowledging his name whilst in the garb he then wore; neither could his feelings of duty acquiesce in his doing so without the permission of his mother. That permission he flattered himself he should obtain; and that, in attire beseeming his station, he should, on the morrow, present himself at the gate of Harcourt House. But the morrow found him in prison, confounded with the culprits who had acted both in the excitement to, and the performance of, the outrages; when the explanation necessary to procure his liberation led to his presentation to the king, who advised his immediate departure for the Continent, as the most effectual means of hushing every unpleasant animadversion upon his thoughtless frolic with associates so unsuited to his rank.

For one year longer St. Aubin remained upon the Continent; but, through the Argus-eyed manœuvring of his mother, never once encountering Lord Harcourt or his daughter, on their progress through Italy. At the expiration of that year, St. Aubin was recalled by the king, and received the appointment of one of the chief pages to Henry, who promised, when he acquired a little more steadiness, to promote him to some higher station.

CHAPTER VIII.

A READY answer of compliance being returned from Lord Harcourt to the king's mandate, the joy almost maddened St. Aubin, who set out for Alba with a command from Henry—who was no patron of long wooing —to marry forthwith, as his presence would be shortly wanting at court to aid in some approaching festivities.

Whether it was that the sombre melancholy of Alba Castle cooled the ardour of St. Aubin's passion; but soon something very like dismay assailed him. Adela no longer possessed the perfection of beauty which had dazzled and fascinated his youthful fancy; for, although the shaft that destroyed her happiness had penetrated her heart ere her second meeting with St. Aubin, and the canker had entered the rose, its blighting influence was not, in that early progress of its effects, perceptible. Now, nearly three years of corroding grief, and months of anxious vigil by the pillow of her suffering father, had cruelly changed the natural loveliness of Lady Adela.

St. Aubin felt conviction that Adela was still as interesting in aspect, amiable, and accomplished as ever; but his heart no longer leaped with joy at the prospect of his union.

A royal command for the nuptials immediately to be celebrated had been sent to Lord Harcourt, and the mandate was complied with as speedily as possible; and St. Aubin, in further obedience to his royal master's wishes, took his bride from the sombre horrors of Alba Castle, very shortly after the sacred knot was tied, to the gay metropolis, where Lord Harcourt promised soon to join them.

At the moment in which the heart-wrung Adela invoked the parting blessing of her sire, the observant Father Hubert read in his patron's countenance an expression of touching sadness, almost bordering on despair. Upon asking Lord Harcourt some questions relating to the subject of arrangements for their journey, his lordship in mournful tones replied:—

" I fear I shall not accomplish this journey to London, my reverend friend, Father Hubert; the mandate for my departure to brighter realms has already arrived. It came through my long-breaking heart when I consigned my ill-fated child to misery by this unlucky marriage. In the very moment when I obeyed the king's command, in the sacrifice of my devoted child, I remarked that he whom we had thus enriched was not content with his precious bride. Oh, holy sir! my sweet, my blighted flower, in her young hour of budding beauty, by the cruelty of that silent uncomplaining heroism which duty long assigned her, is foredoomed to be scorned like a noxious weed. Oh, Father Hubert, my child, my child!" And Lord Harcourt burst into an agony of tears, and sobbed piteously.

Father Hubert, on whom the fascinating manners and amiable charac ˉ ter of St. Aubin had made a most favourable impression, now strove, in every kind tone of sympathising feeling, to dissipate such inauspicious predictions; but in vain.

"Oh! had I but known St. Aubin's indifference to my Adela, ere the fatal knot was tied," continued the agitated father, " I would have snatched the hapless victim from her dreadful fate, even at the altar, and have then with gladness expiated my daring on the headsman's block ! You, Father Hubert, who have beheld Adela's endurance of mental sufferings, like to a smiling martyr on wing for her native heaven —you, who have seen how she endured the unkindly petulance of her peevish sire, until, by the never-clouded sun of her tenderness and duty, she warmed me into all that could beseem a grateful and adoring parent —you cannot feel amazed if my heart should quail at this final destruction of her earthly happiness."

Feeling, through every fibre of his sinking frame, that the leveller of all was hovering near him, Lord Harcourt wasted not one precious moment ere he effected all things within his power for the temporal advantage and security of his child and her descendants; and this important business satisfactorily arranged, his lordship devoutly turned his thoughts to sacred themes, and shortly after closed his life of sorrow and disappointment.

Lady Adela was scarcely settled in Harcourt House, ere an express arrived from Father Hubert to prepare her for the dissolution of her parent. Adela would have flown on the wings of ardent feeling, to take the station of duty and affection by the couch of her beloved father, had not St. Aubin desired her compliance with the advice of her reverend correspondent, not to set out for Alba until summoned by him : but that summons came not ; for the next express conveyed intelligence that all was over.

The grief of the new Countess of Harcourt (an hereditary right established the succession in the female line in failure of male issue) for the individual loss of her parent was poignant : but his last illness and death occurring when bereft of all kindred consolation, added agony to her sorrow; and she had no one near to yield her comfort.

Adela had been loved—to adoration loved—by De Lacy : and thus early initiated in the tenderness of the passion which she had inspired, she soon detected its non-existence in the bosom of her husband; and whilst endeavouring to call up all the forces of her fortitude upon this discovery, to bear her still on with firmness through a continued life of uncomplaining misery, she yet hoped and prayed that St. Aubin might

not betray this mortifying indifference to all around them : but, too soon,
the alacrity with which he entered into every project which called him
from her society led her to the conviction that this inattention would
soon become evident to all observers.

Although Adela could no longer boast the brilliancy of beauty which
had captivated the youthful fancy of her husband, she was still lovely.
St. Aubin, alas ! neither hoped nor wished to admire Adela more.
Lord Fitzstephen, with enmity to the house of Mandeville for its scorn of
his alliance, and envy to St. Aubin for obtaining the rich prize he
coveted, determined to make the union an inauspicious one ; and, for
this purpose, entered into a combination with the abbess and nuns of
St. Mildred, who had also imbibed enmity to Lord Harcourt and his
daughter, because the munificent donation which had formerly been
placed in their hands for charitable purposes had lately flowed through
other channels into the habitations of the sick and needy ; and impatiently they had awaited an opportunity of revenge.   Upon the death of
Father Richard, which had some time since occurred, a promotion in
the clerical establishment at Alba had occasioned a vacancy, which was
filled up by a priest recommended by the abbess of St. Mildred named
Nicoli.   Upon the arrival of St. Aubin at Alba, to wed the heiress,
this wily Nicoli soon insinuated himself into the good graces of the
guileless St. Aubin ; and under pretence of strenuous efforts to strike
out amusement for the poor moped youth, inveigled him to St. Mildred's, to view the curiosities which the church contained, and from
the church led him into the repository, where the various works of the
nuns were exhibited for sale.   The two old members of the sisterhood,
who appeared as venders of these ingenious performances, wore the
aspect of Sibyllæ, and were not unlike them in manner too ; for soon,
almost as if writing it on the mysterious leaf, they began to gabble
about St. Aubin's future fortunes, and as if he had fascinated them into
sudden anxiety for his happiness, threw out many ambiguous hints, as
if they more hoped than expected felicity to be his through a union
with Adela of Alba : then, as if in regret that they had suffered this
anxiety to beguile them into betraying secrets, endeavouring to unsay
what they had hinted at, in that artful way in which more disclosures
seemed to drop inadvertently through that confusion which a sense of
having acted wrong had awakened, until they manœuvred to allow it to
appear that Lady Adela had been engaged in necromantic practices :
that she had used Sir Hugo cruelly ; and that it had been rumoured
her conduct in prudence had not been too scrupulous.

St. Aubin, perfectly guileless in his own nature, was little aware of
the duplicity with which the world abounded.   He knew that the
recluse of monasteries were prone to superstition ; and that, if they
did not absolutely believe in the miraculous themselves, they sedulously
endeavoured to establish it in the faith of others ; and, not feeling any
tendency towards becoming a proselyte to this species of doctrine, he
inwardly laughed to scorn the supposition of Lady Adela ever having

THE FATAL GULF.

been engaged in forming magic spells—unless such, indeed, as she had performed upon himself in their first two interviews. But the latter insinuation of these venal tools of defamation fell with surer aim ; and, trembling with apprehension that something must be true of what had been betrayed to him, he complied with the summons of Father Nicoli (who affected to appear much distressed at such untoward communications, to the parlour of the abbess, where he had been invited to partake of some refreshment.

The lady abbess of St. Mildred was in the zenith of superior beauty, and the possessor of captivating manners ; concealing not only art, but vices, under the most prepossessing form of guileless truth, striking elegance, and surpassing mental acquirements ; and, as if she feared her own attractions might not prove efficient for the purpose of beguiling, she had selected the beautiful Isabel for her companion ; under the pretence of Isabel's amiable anxiety for an introduction to him, who was so shortly to be allied to the fumily which so benevolently protected her.

St. Aubin, from having received his education principally under his mother's care, had naturally imbibed much of the effeminacy of bestowing too much consequence upon exterior excellence. Beauty and grace were therefore, in his estimation, the superlatives of human perfection ; so that even in the first interview, these dazzling infatuators penetrated with their bewitching spells so deeply and firmly into his admiration, that, whilst he remained in their neighbourhood, not one hour which he could extricate from the society of Lady Adela, and the gloom of her father's castle, but was devoted to his new fascinators ; who, beside this exploit of alluring his fealty from his destined bride to themselves, artfully contrived, from time to time, whilst as if in the act of eulogising Lady Adela, to drop some suspicious word of counter import, then hastily to abandon it, without its termination, as if recollections had fortunately come in time only to save some fearful truth against Lady Adela transpiring : thus they completely succeeded in adding force to the suspicions which the nuns first had awakened of Lady Adela not being faultless, until at length nothing but apprehension of the fearful wrath of the arbitrary monarch, who had willed this alliance for him, could have prevented the recoiling St. Aubin from withdrawing from this engagement ; and, influenced by these subverted feelings and disgusts, he had reluctantly wedded the inestimable heiress of Harcourt.

The pleasure-loving monarch, not brooking a postponement to his pending jousts and revels through respect to the remains of a suspected peer, peremptorily commanded St. Aubin not to attend the obsequies of Lord Harcourt ; but the heart-wrung Adela would have fled to Alba, even unaccompanied by her truant husband, had not the shock thus added to her affliction, in this irreverence to the remains of her noble father, confined her to a bed of sickness ; and, when sufficiently recovered to make any removal practicable, she was surprised by a proposition of removing immediately to the coast of Kent, for the benefit of the sea breezes.

This pretended kindness was but the delusion of political deception. The interview which afterwards took place at Guisnes, between Henry and Francis, was now in the contemplation of the monarch, who having formed hopes, in national pride, of effecting the magnificent scene in England, he and Wolsey judged it necessary to have some individual competent to the undertaking to spend a few weeks on the coast, to make observation upon every spot of land opposite to France, to determine upon the capabilities which it possessed for such a measure; and none appearing so equal to the purpose as St. Aubin, who possessed unrivalled taste in every species of pageant, he was nominated for the task: and secrecy being wished for by the royal projector, the state of Lady Harcourt's health was hailed as an admirable excuse for her husband's sojourn upon the coast; and in the then comparatively small town of Dover they were almost immediately established, with the accompaniment of another invalid in Lady Darlington.

Every hour that Adela now lived she more deeply felt convinced that domestic happiness was not for her. In vain were the most tender attentions paid by her to Lady Darlington, for they seemed to have no effect upon either mother or son; but their influence upon poor Adela herself too soon became apparent. To evince respect and attention to the kind parent of her husband she had exerted herself prematurely, after her recent severe indisposition; and, consequently, she once more was consigned to her chamber, there uninterruptedly to nourish the recollection of her varied griefs, without one sympathising being near her, save poor Maud. But soon, too soon, an addition to their party was most unexpectedly presented in the beautiful Isabel, who announced that her dear benefactress having promised, when a fair opportunity offered for her conveyance to her protection, she would send for her to tarry awhile; and two of the boarders having been summoned from St. Mildred's to their home at Paris, she had seized the opportunity thus unexpectedly offered, and had travelled with them to join her dear kind friend, whom she had longed so ardently to see.

But her longing ardour evinced much temperance in its gratification; for, after the first interview, very short ones sufficed for Isabel, who soon announced, "that Lady Darlington had taken a strange fancy to her style of reading, and wished her to read constantly to her." Lady Harcourt would not interfere with any wish of Lady Darlington; and although she felt grieved that her dear *protégée* should at length be under the same roof with her, and she not to be indulged with her society, uttered not one murmur.

But Maud could have murmured, and that with every effusion of indignation against the ingratitude of Isabel, had not anxiety for the peace of her dear lady kept her silent.

For about half an hour each day this young and wily deceiver read to, or otherwise amused, Lady Darlington; and the rest of her time was wholly devoted to St. Aubin, who, ere her arrival, had been oppressed with *ennui*. Now Isabel was the favoured of all his excursions, and yielded beauty and captivation to every spot they visited together; and so complete a fascinator St. Aubin found her, that when his hapless wife was once more able to quit her chamber, it could not be concealed from her observation, no more than from that of all around them, that Isabel had become her potent and determined rival.

CHAPTER IX.

No sense of duty, nor of forbearance, could have operated in detaining Lady Harcourt much longer in Dover, to sanction, by her presence, that imprudence which had become the public theme; and she was only pausing to arrange some method of withdrawing herself and *protégée* to Alba without hostilities, when a personage arrived to change the current of the tide which had threatened to overwhelm her. Gilbert Fitzstephen, next brother to the baron of that name, a handsome, dissipated young man, with little property, and no expectations, made his appearance in Dover, to claim the promised hand of Isabel; whose project for quitting St. Mildred's had originally been for the purpose of operating upon the partiality of her benefactress, into granting her a nobler provision than that arranged for her by Lord Harcourt, with her permission to wed Gilbert Fitzstephen.

The enamoured Gilbert had arranged to follow her to Dover; and scarcely had he arrived there, when the palfrey of Isabel, gaily trapped ready for her mounting, passed the hostelry where he had lodged himself, and drew remarks from those around him, which filled his bosom with the most jealous apprehensions, and induced him to present himself, without a moment for reflection, before the astonished Adela, to state his serious engagement with Isabel.

Upon Isabel's return from her excursion, she positively denied her betrothment; and so aroused the indignation of St. Aubin, at such presumptuous falsehood, that the most fatal consequences would probably have ensued, had not a royal mandate opportunely arrived to call him on the instant to Greenwich.

A moment's delay in obedience to the royal mandate might prove more than his head was worth; to take Isabel with him, impracticable; and to leave her in the same spot with the arrogant pretender, were tortures to St. Aubin: his only consolation was, to obtain assurances from the ready promise-maker, Isabel, " that no lures of the presumptuous

Fitzstephen should ensnare her into becoming his;" and to issue his mandate to Adela, "not to sanction the pretensions of a man for her *protégée*, whose family had been deemed, by her own honourable father, unworthy of allegiance with the children of integrity."

Adela had neither wish nor intention of sacrificing her *protégée* to any man: but after her husband's solemn mandate, she declined all further communication, either by interview or letter, with the importunate Fitzstephen; who, however, very shortly after the departure of St. Aubin, was most unexpectedly furnished with an auxiliary of resistless force for winning the inconstant Isabel, in the intelligence of the death of his elder brother; and no sooner was this event communicated to Isabel, than she commenced her serious calculations upon whether becoming a baroness immediately might not prove a wiser speculation than being the mistress of St. Aubin.

St. Aubin, impatient to terminate the hopes of his rival, made no delay, after his departure from Greenwich was permitted, in flying back to Dover, where he was received by the wily Isabel with the most flattering welcome, and parted from her at night as her sanctioned lover; but on the morrow the deceiver had vanished; eloped with the new lord to the Continent, there to effect a marriage whenever the peculiar circumstances attendant upon her birth could render it lawful; and having embarked in the night, on board a smuggling vessel, under that veil of secrecy and caution which contraband traffic rendered necessary, all clue to their route was effectually destroyed.

Isabel artfully fabricated a pathetic epistle to St. Aubin, stating, "that gratitude to the Harcourt family had led her from the man of her heart's affection, to become the wife of a person she could never love, for the conscientious purpose of restoring peace to the bosom of her benefactress." This epistle Isabel left on her dressing-table, directed to St. Aubin.

The valet of St. Aubin delivered the packet the moment he was summoned to attend him in his dressing-room; and St. Aubin, having dismissed his attendant, that he might read without an observer this unexpected communication, had no one near to save him from falling to the ground; where, with every faculty suspended, he sank on perusing the intelligence of Isabel being lost to him for ever.

The deep groan which preceded, and the noise that accompanied, the fall of St. Aubin, drew Adela in alarm into the apartment, when her piercing shriek, penetrating through the small dwelling, drew the valet promptly to her side, to aid in the recovery of his master.

The letter of Isabel, still grasped in the clenched hand of St. Aubin, made too conspicuous a figure in the scene to escape the observation and recognition of his wife, who, disdaining to penetrate the secret which evidently had occasioned this alarming effect, and shrinking from the possibility of ever being suspected upon the subject, caused the valet to secure it before the arrival of the leech, who found it necessary to open a vein, ere St. Aubin evinced symptoms of returning sense. But re-animation only recalled him to a sense of suffering, which in a few hours reduced him to a bed of sickness. Adela never left her station by his pillow, day nor night, although his wild ravings were incessantly of his devoted attachment to her rival.

During three weeks, which passed heavily on ere St. Aubin's fever came to its crisis, the death and burial of Lady Dar-lington had taken place; for the elopement of Isabel, and its fearful effect upon her son, having been incautiously disclosed to her, brought on a fatal attack of paralysis.

On the first dawn of St. Aubin's reason, he observed his now hated wife at her anxious station; and he would have fled in detesta-tion from her presence, or commanded her from his, had he then pos-sessed power to effect either purpose: but thus compelled to endure her presence, it was gradually unfolded to his sensibility that by Adela's hand alone comfort was ever conveyed to him, that her tender assiduities never slumbered, though the hireling nurse snored; and these observations, allowed through intervals from the slumbers of his abating malady, horror at the presence of Adela completely ceased; and the first effort he achieved, to evince consciousness of her pre-sence, was a gentle pressure of her hand.

This unexpected symptom of affection penetrated with such touching effect to the susceptibility of Adela, that tears burst forth in torrents. Her tears were gifted with sympathetic influence, for they drew sponta-neously a copious flood from the eyes of St. Aubin, and with such be-neficial tendency, that his long-suspended faculty of speaking was restored, but to little present purpose, for what could he say to Adela? In a moment of Adela's absence, he inquired for Isabel's letter, and learned from the valet "where, by order of the countess, it had been secured from all inspectors;" and this trait of honourable feeling pe-netrated so deeply, that when the hand of Adela again came in contact with his own, he pressed it to his lips with grateful fervour; and, in a moment after, in a tone of thrilling sensibility, expressed the assurance that he felt of her not having allowed his poor mother to be neglected during his unfortunate illness.

These words struck with such an electric shock to the heart of Adela, that the susceptible St. Aubin felt it rebound through her hand to his own heart. Instantly his bed perceptibly quivered under him.

A conference with Father James confirmed too fatally all his sa forebodings; and his intense affliction for his mother called his me-lancholy thoughts from dwelling exclusively upon his loss of the worth-less Isabel.

When the tender care of Adela became no longer necessary, with delicate attention to what she conceived would be her husband's wish, she withdrew from a constant station by his pillow, but inexplicably to himself her absence grieved him; and whether from selfish motives, which led him to believe that there was only safety for him in her constant attendance, or that feeling himself now alone in the world, he wished to find solace in her gentle friendship, he summoned her so frequently to resume her old seat, that she at length seldom quitted him; when mutually compassionating each other for the individual misery they had each been doomed to suffer from inauspicious love, for the unfavourable construction given by the nuns of St. Mildred to the termination of Adela's betrothment were fading into total oblivion in the mind of St. Aubin, the kindlings of pity called up a softening feeling in their growing friendship, which might have shortly ripened into conjugal tenderness, had it not been for the reciprocal belief, that the heart of each was irrevocably pre-occupied.

St. Aubin, at length, again visited court, when the king perceiving his once mirthful countenance veiled in sadness, readily yielded him permission to remove to Alba, where he continued until after his amiable countess had presented him with a son and heir, when the title of Baron Harcourt, being now his right by usage, and that of earl through the original hereditary grant, he repaired to London to take his seat in the House of Peers. But as he journeyed his first stage on this route from Alba, he encountered one of the fathers attached to St. Mildred's, also on horseback. After riding the same road for some time, Lord Harcourt summoned resolution to inquire from him, " If any intelligence had reached their community relative to Isabel?" When the communicative priest replied in the affirmative, stating, " That she was yet abroad with her husband; that she had become a mother to a lovely female infant; but had encountered severe pecuniary difficulties through the gambling and other dissipated propensities of her lord, until the Countess Harcourt, hearing of her distress, had forwarded to her a noble sum, which she had long since obtained from her late father, and kept by her for the purpose of presenting to her *protégée*, should she marry with her approbation.

The first impulse of Lord Harcourt's feeling upon this intelligence was to gallop back to Alba Castle, and clasp Adela to his grateful bosom for this noble conduct to Isabel, whom the voice of contrast whispered painfully did not deserve it from Adela. But a moment's reflection led him onward.

When our new Lord Harcourt arrived in London, he found the whole court in eager preparation for the meeting of the French and English sovereigns at Guisne, and as the melancholy of his voice and countenance had considerably subsided, and he possessed ample power to make a magnificent addition in his suite to the imposing spectacle in arrangement, Henry commanded his attendance upon this occasion. For the first time, Lord Harcourt felt a mandate from his sovereign a painful grievance; since it was to separate him for an indefinite time from his adored boy: nor did he feel quite contented at the idea of a lengthened separation from Adela herself.

The chaste taste and munificent spirit of Lady Harcourt, notwithstanding the obstacles of distance, regulated the preparations of her lord for the splendid regal interview which at length took place; and as soon as Lord Harcourt was emancipated from attendance upon his sovereign, and received the kind caution, " To live warily after his late expenditure," he hastened to Alba: and, although feeling no necessity for living warily, he felt rejoiced to have the power of living quietly in his own castle, where, with transport, he folded his lovely babe to his throbbing bosom; and embraced the countess, whom he thought must have been absolutely practising necromancy with her aspect during his absence; so much had maternal happiness, and exemption from connubial mortification and anxiety, improved her beauty; and often as he looked upon his lovely wife, he believed that could she be exonerated from every impropriety relative to Sir Hugo de Lacy, that it would prove no difficult task to wean his heart from Isabel.

But, alas! poor Adela was not doomed to continue long in the pleasant path that seemed to be leading her to felicity; for, as on all prior occasions when she firmly trusted she had entered the road to certain happiness, she found it terminate in misery. The idol heir sickened and died; and the almost distracted parents were separated in the moment of their calamity, by a royal mandate for Lord Harcourt to repair to Rome, to be present when the Dean of Windsor presented his majesty's treatise against Martin Luther to the Pope; and to let his majesty know, truly and honestly, what Leo and his conclave thought, or said, relative to this composition. Nothing for the peace of this now almost tenderly attached pair could have proved more inauspicious; for in Rome his lordship unfortunately encountered the baneful Isabel, matured into dazzling beauty; her skill in accomplishments improved by Italian instruction to fascinating perfection.

Upon the susceptibilities of Lord Harcourt she promptly exercised her seductive powers, and he as promptly fell a ready victim to her lures. His heart again became all her own—and soon his purse also; and, notwithstanding his copious flow of wealth from England, he could scarcely supply the demands of the unprincipled Isabel.

Unfortunately for the infatuated Harcourt, he still was detained by his mission, in the spot which Isabel illumined; and coldly he at length received the intelligence from Rome, "that Lady Harcourt was again a parent; and that the young stranger was a daughter."

The madly devoted Harcourt sent, with his heartless contratulations upon her safety, a request to Adela, for their infant daughter to be named Isabel, after the most admired woman of the age; and to this request his heart-wrung wife replied, "that ere his request reached Alba, in full belief that she was anticipating his wishes, she had had his daughter baptized by the name borne by a woman deservedly admired in the age which she had adorned—Louise, after his own inestimable mother."

This reply struck upon the gratitude and conscience of Lord Harcourt so forcibly, that he would have set out for home immediately, had not his actions been under political control. But a few interviews with Lady Fitzstephen obliterated these feelings; so that, when at length his recall from Italy arrived, it proved little less than annihilation to tear himself from Isabel, whom he madly promised to make speedy arrangements, out of his ample stores, for her husband to return with her to England.

Consciousness of ingratitude to the inestimable Adela, to whom he owed all that influx of wealth which he had lavished so reprehensibly upon her infatuating rival, caused him tardily to direct his movements homeward ; and though when he did at last arrive at Alba he acknowledged to himself his spouse looked most lovely, yet the more dazzling charms of Isabel spell-bound all auspicious effect upon his admiration ; and in that state of perverted feeling, which reprehensible attachments invariably occasion, almost pronounced poor Adela a culprit for looking well after the calamity her maternal happiness had sustained scarcely one year since ; not once accusing his own transgressing looks, or reflecting how completely he had ceased to recollect and bewail his lost child in the society of Isabel. But, returned to his own castle, he never ceased to remember and lament him ; the new infant, the heroine of these pages, completely failing to awaken paternal interest : for, unluckily, Lady Louise had not, like her late brother, personal attractions—for she seemed a mere ball of fat and good temper : and her dissatisfied father pronounced she had neither nose nor eyes discernible, and turned in horror from her, even as she smiled and crowed her tiny allurements.

With sorrow poor Adela perceived it, and her own diminution in the esteem of her lord ; esteem she despaired of ever now regaining, as his lordship seldom yielded her any opportunity, spending his time chiefly at York, or at Fitzstephen Castle, arranging for the performance of his promise to Isabel ; but which his susceptible feelings of honour led him to find a comfortless pursuit, and at length compelled him to relinquish altogether ; for upon investigating all the difficulties of the case, he felt conviction that nothing short of the direct robbery of Adela and her progeny could enable the Fitzstephens to return to their native country, and establish them in their baronial castle ; when in despair at this bitter disappointment, he daily quitted his home to brood in lonely walks and rides upon his wretchedness.

But these rides and walks were through those paths most likely to regain for Adela that prized ground she feared for ever lost ; since, go whithersoever, or encounter whomsoever, he might, affecting anecdotes in proof of the beauties of his wife's heart perpetually assailed him ; and, day after day, he at length returned to Alba, with looks and tones softening once more to tenderness : and just as the merry Louise had attained her eighteenth month, without having been able to crow, or caper, or manœuvre herself by any infantile stratagem, into the better graces of her father, and without having expanded much more promise of beauty, another blossom was added to the daily opening flowers of conjugal felicity in Alba Castle, by the birth of a lovely boy.

CHAPTER X.

THE birth of this son and heir was hailed with rapture by his parents, and the animated little Louise shrieked with delight when she firs beheld, and was permitted to kiss, her brother.

The child was hourly advancing in strength and beauty, and his mother in the tender friendship of his father, when intelligence arrived of the death of Baron Fitzstephen in an affray at a gaming-house in Rome. The pang conveyed to the heart of Lord Harcourt on Isabel

being free, whilst he was fettered, foreboded nothing propitious to the cause of Adela: and this pang had many a successor, when the abbess of St. Mildred's conveyed a letter from the beautiful widow to him, in which she stated herself and child to be left in absolute penury; for that even the *trifle* which Lady Harcourt had sent to her had been appropriated by her lord to his own dissipated purposes: and whilst writhing in agony, inflicted by the tone of this artful epistle, his lordship was compelled, by some domestic occurrence, to enter the presence of her he was meditating a flight from, that he might rescue Isabel from the fangs of poverty, and place her and her child in safe protection.

Lord Harcourt perceived that Adela was agitated, and that his unexpected entrance had led her to the effort of subduing tears. After a moment's struggle with her feelings, Adela addressed her lord; but whilst she did so, delicately averted her glances as she spoke of Isabel, and informed him, that she had received intimation from the abbess of the great affliction the child of her early affection was placed in by the death of her unworthy husband.

"You, my dear," she continued in a thrilling tone of sweetness, "can manage better in aiding poor Isabel than I, and assuaging her sorrow. Perhaps, through your influence, our ambassador at Rome might do all things for you in accordance with our intent. Or, some one express from us would perhaps better grace our sympathy. Father Hubert, as our envoy, would be a proper person to go; and would do all that was needful for Isabel's comfort and consolation."

Adela could not utter this kindness with a steady voice: forgiving mercy almost overpowered her melting cadences; but when she came to her concluding sentence, she was clasped by her agitated husband to his bosom; and, without power or inclination to restrain them, he wept over her the flowing tears of all the feelings she had touched; and for many minutes Adela wept with him.

At length Adela, starting from the trembling arms of Harcourt, brought water to revive him; and now, in continuance of her long habit of sparing the feelings of others, by concealing her own, sent her agitation from the surface to the confines of her generous heart, and gently said, "Perhaps ere you decide on our plan of assisting Lady Fitzstephen, you may deem it more to your wishes to consult with the abbess of St. Mildred's; if so, pray seek her."

"I will advise with none but my angelic wife!" exclaimed Harcourt. "Let Father Hubert wend his way to Rome, my Adela; he will do all that beseemeth him on the poor sufferer's behalf, with the same delicacy, faith, and honour, that yourself would."

"Whither shall he take the poor mourner? What habitation is meet for her, Harcourt, in her widowed state?—To—to—" and the voice of Adela faltered, in union with the tumultuous bounding of her heart: "to St. Mildred's, or whither, my good lord?"

Every fibre in Harcourt's frame now shook with agitation, and so did Adela. Harcourt snatched up the cruise of water, swallowed a large gulp, then threw himself into the arms of his wife, and clasped them around him, as if he thus himself constituted her his shield from error; and then with some difficulty articulated his desire, which was for Father Hubert to attend Lady Fitzstephen to Trent, where an aunt of her late husband was superior of a monastery; and which he thought would be her most eligible place of sojourn for the two first years of her widowhood.

Adela, feeling as if her rescue from destruction had been now achieved by her husband's magnanimous victory over his own wishes, pressed his hand in tender gratitude to her lips, and silently withdrew to prepare Father Hubert for his unexpected embassy. In a very few hours he departed, charged with a kind letter from Adela, and one befitting the husband of such a wife from Lord Harcourt to Lady Fitzstephen, and in due time arrived at his place of destination. He found the disconsolate and pennyless widow in a superb villa about a mile out of the city, surrounded by magnificence and luxury, and looking as if no "—— worm i' the bud fed on her damask cheek," or was likely so to do.

Father Hubert delivered his credentials, and a heavy purse of marcs, which the countess had sent for the present use of Isabel. Lady Fitzstephen requested two days to arrange for her departure for Trent, and appointed the hour upon which she would be in readiness to accompany the good Father to the protection of her deceased husband's aunt; and gave him various addresses where he was to pay different sums of money, to enable her to quit Rome without molestation: but when the holy man returned to her villa, according to Lady Fitzstephen's own arrangement, the *ignis fatuus* was gone; having left a letter to inform him that she had fled to an asylum more likely to effect the restoration of her happiness than that appointed for her by his noble patrons.

The place of this arch-designer's destination was St. Mildred's monastery! and, ere poor Father Hubert's statement of how she had absconded could arrive at Alba, a letter from the fugitive herself was delivered to Lord Harcourt, dated St. Mildred's, stating, " That distraction at his cruelty, in consigning her to banishment from that individual society in which alone existence was prized by her, had led her to use the purse bestowed in ostentatious charity upon her by the happy Lady Harcourt in bringing her on the wings of affection into Yorkshire, to ascertain if lingering death was to be her doom, in conviction that he had ceased to love her."

How the melting pathos of this artful composition operated upon the heart of Lord Harcourt must be left at present for conjecture to determine; but the magic of her love epistles assailed him every hour this day, and attracted answers back to her at St. Mildred's until eventide, when his lordship, with the appearance almost of a distracted man, set out on horseback from Alba; and in about two hours after his departure from the castle, a letter arrived from his lordship to the alarmed Adela, to whom the secret of Lady Fitzstephen's arrival at St. Mildred's that morning had been revealed by the mischief-loving Father Nicoli.

From the moment this unwelcome intelligence had been imparted by Father Nicoli to the countess, trembling agitation and touching sadness marked her aspect and her manner, until after the arrival of her lord's express, which seemed to convey some most efficacious balm to her tranquillity; for, after a short retirement to her oratory, she appeared to all around her as absolutely treading in air; and ere Maud took leave of her beloved lady for the night, poor Adela confided to her, that she, her children, and her favourite attendants, were immediately to set out with her lord upon the Continent, to travel for three years.

Adela had lately found it an efficacious measure to walk before breakfast, when the tide permitted, upon the beach, which formed one boundary of the Alba domain. It therefore awakened no surprise amongst the household, her setting out alone, the morning after the sudden departure of her lord, upon her usual pedestrianism; nor was the procrastination of her absence observed, until the volatile Lady Louise began to evince impatience for her mother's caresses; when Maud, who had been extremely busy, making preparations for the meditated tour, was aroused to wonder her lady had not yet returned; and which wonder led to a sudden recollection that this was the first morning of an expected spring tide—that probably the swell had come unexpectedly upon her, and compelled her sojourn on some exalted rock for safety.

The gentlemen of the household and attendants, upon this recollection, instantly sallied forth to extricate their idolised lady from the inconvenience, and perhaps danger, of her situation; some descending to the rocks from higher cliffs, while others set out in boats upon the ocean, in case that by this means her extrication might be more conveniently and speedily effected: but no where could they discern her whom they anxiously sought; no call, no shout, attracted the response they panted for; and the most agonising alarms were at length awakened.

Nor were these alarms without foundation. Every man who could procure a horse to mount, galloped off in wild affright to spread the alarm, and seek information relative to her they sought; whilst those who could not, remained near the shore, in agonies of expectation upon what the ebbing or the subsequent returning tide might bring of fatal intelligence. Far and wide the alarm was spread—a few hours found the whole country in a tumult: the sheriff, the nobles, the religious, the yeomen, all turned out to seek, to trace, to find her whom all esteemed; whilst her own household and dependants were like distracted parents, wives, husbands, children, seeking and lamenting their beloved lost lady; and those affecting deeds of charity and kindness, which Adela's right hand had never revealed to her left, now were blazoned forth as trophies ready to adorn her tomb.

The tide ebbed, and in terror proofs were sought, which all recoiled from finding. A shoe, a sleeve, and a veil, were discovered; and the heart-broken Maud, ascertaining their having formed part of the countess's attire when she had set out upon her fatal walk, the sad confirmation of the fate of Adela was believed by all her mourners—and these were all the county, save those whom the walls of St. Mildred's monasteries then encompassed.

From this moment nets were laid along the coast, and mourning, anxious groups appeared, almost stationary, morning, noon, and night, in the sad hope of the coming waves restoring their lost treasure, to receive the rites of Christian sepulture. But the realising of this sad hope was deferred for nearly three weeks; when, on the return of an early morning tide, the body of a female was discovered floating on the deep; and as each coming wave brought it nearer and still nearer to the shore, the lamentations of anticipating sorrow sounded forth in touching dirge, and the sympathetic bells of St. Mildred's were almost instantaneous in their loud and dolefully tolled response.

The body reached the shore; and those whose hearts bled at receiving this afflicting restitution found the revered corse so decomposed that no trace of the Countess of Harcourt could be discovered; but every part of the dress, which had not been too much destroyed for recognition, yielded incontrovertible testimony that this was too surely her.

The coffins had been prepared in expectation of this possible restitution; but, to the grief of all, the revered remains were, through necessity, soldered up without the usual ceremonies. The coffins were laid in state, and every preparation for the funeral arranged in readiness for the momentarily looked for arrival of Lord Harcourt, after whom an express with the melancholy tidings had been forwarded to London, whither it was supposed he had gone from Alba. His lordship's eldest brother and Father Hubert arrived, but no Harcourt; and the intelligence brought by the holy man gave assurance that his lordship could not be in Yorkshire in time for the interment, since the reverend father had encountered Lord Harcourt in France, on his way to Geneva, whither he had been commissioned by his lordship to conduct the countess and her babes, without delay, to join him.

Upon this information Lord Darlington took upon himself to act in conjunction with Father Hubert, who had been her ladyship's trustee, and one of the late lord's executors; and with grief of heart the sorrow-stricken preceptor of the inestimable Adela set about this afflicting duty; in doing which he had perpetually to encounter her, whom, in the existing state of his feelings, he most recoiled from,—the ignis fatuus who had eluded him in Italy, and whom the shrewd Hubert believed was acting for deep effect in her usual path of wily artifice, which had now placed her in Alba Castle.

The deep designer Isabel had, upon the first alarm for the fate of Adela, presented herself before the gate of Alba Castle, in a state of apparent agitation befitting the anxiety of the moment, obttained entrance, and established herself in the nursery; where she declared, that should the reported late melancholy bearings of the inestimable countess have led her to any act of self-destruction, she should strive to repay in some degree the debt of gratitude she owed her dear protectress, by devoting herself to her two helpless babes; and this intention Lady Fitzstephen soon found occasion for pronouncing herself called upon to perform; for Adela had too surely disappeared; and upon this trying occasion the tenderness of Isabel's attention to the suffering Edward, called forth the admiration of all but those who knew her.

The little Louise, also, it was the object of this deep designer to attract by kindness, not then in the secret that poor Louise's attachments were unlikely to influence her father: but Louise soon perceiving this obliging lady procured for her every thing she asked for, took it into imagination, that, through the same power, she could bring her mother to her. Every moment, therefore, in which she could attract the attention of this stranger, her cry became more and more importunate and affecting—" To go for her mother !—To bring her mother back to Louise and brother !"—until the child at length thought that though the lady could, she would not, bring back her mother: and in consequence of this belief, her resentment awakened dislike to her, which unfortunately became mutual; and, in the mind of Lady Fitzstephen, assumed a deadly hue—menacing the future happiness of the innocent babe.

Although her ladyship could not deceive Father Hubert or Maud, she completely succeeded in convincing Lord Darlington that she was an angel in a human mould; and, in her affected artlessness, detecting her ardent attachment to Lord Harcourt, he pronounced his brother fortunate, since, through this attachment, he could give his children another celestial being to yield a mother's care; and, in his despatches to Lord Harcourt, failed not to paint her conduct in the most fascinating form.

The daughter of Isabel had her post assigned her, too, in the drama of attraction. She had been instructed to find her way into Alba Castle, bathed in tears at separation from her mother; and when established there, to win the affection of all around her by her sweet docile manners; and, finally, to profess perfect adoration of Harcourt's son, and to exert all her winning wiles to render their attachment reciprocal. This miniature lord seemed to enter very amicably into the views and wishes of Lady Fitzstephen, for he took very peaceably to the partialities with which she toiled for his being inspired: but not so Lady Louise; for, after having appeared for some days quietly to endure the soft and gentle coaxings of this new companion, she suddenly evinced such unequivocal hostility to her very approach, that at length Lord Darlington ordered a separate suite of chambers to be established instantly for the wild savage Louise, apart from her toward brother and his kind friends; and where possibly, under the control of Maud, who seemed so strangely partial to the young vixen, she might at length be tamed into something civilised.

As Lord Darlington was not tardy in making his admiration known to the infant coquet, Isabel, although not little a envious of her child's attractions, determined to turn this favourable impression to advantage, by interesting his lordship for her future prospects, which were menaced by the next heir to the title and estates of her late husband, upon the plea of some informalities attending the marriage of her parents.

The romantic speculations which filled the mind of Lord Darlington relative to this juvenile captivator, enlisted him at once a zealous agent in her cause; and, ere his departure from Alba, he arranged with Isabel, that they should remove ere long to the Bower, his lordship's seat in Middlesex, where his eldest sister, who had recently become a widow, at present resided with him; and where, from its vicinity to the capital, they could conveniently arrange all necessary legal measures for the preservation of the young baroness's birthright.

This arrangement was therefore, without much delay, effected; and through it Lady Fitzstephen doubted not she should shortly re-enter Alba Castle, as successor to her benefactress, under the auspices of

Lord Harcourt's family : and at the Bower she found all things in conformity to her wishes, except that Lord Harcourt remained upon the Continent upwards of a year after the sad catastrophe of Adela's death had been announced to him, so desultory in his movements that none could succeed in a premeditated encounter with him ; and when he did at length join the long-expecting party, it was evident to all that he had been more than a nominal mourner.

To reanimate the evidently weakened passion of Lord Harcourt became the fixed determination of the mortified and angry Isabel ; who although she had successfully fascinated his brother and sister into potent auxiliaries, found it no easy achievement to rekindle a flame once so ardent : but not until the full expiration of his second year of mourning would he lead her to the altar ; and although at length united to the woman whom he had for years adored, the union did not appear to restore him to happiness. A sad and solemn expression sat on his naturally cheerful countenance ; and if by chance it disappeared, its absence was but momentary.

CHAPTER XI.

At the period in which Lord Harcourt had attended the regal interview at Guisine, a romantic adventure, whilst in full chivalric influence upon his feelings, led his lordship to pledge his honour as a knight that he would, when called upon, take a singularly situated male orphan under his protection, to be educated with his own son. " This orphan boy," his informant stated, " was of noble descent; but so mysteriously menaced, that those who had solemnly sworn to protect him from the sanguinary dagger of an hereditary foe dared not detain him under their own care, as that would inevitably lead to discovery and destruction ; but that under the fostering wing of Lord Harcourt suspicion of his identity would be defeated, and an unoffending innocent saved from pitiless immolation."

Scarcely had this promise passed his lips ere his lordship felt repentant ; and the more he contemplated the subject, the more dissatisfied he became with his hasty promise, since alarm mingled with conviction that at least he had been rashly imprudent : for should this child of mystery turn out to be, what was not improbable, an offset of the Plantagenets, therefore noxious to the Tudors—united as he was, although through the king's own management, with a family whose loyalty had been for some time suspected—what a flood of troubled. waters might he not thus, by his chivalric pity, have turned into a ready course for overwhelming him and his ; nor could the ingenuous declaration which had assailed his vanity, through flattering homage to his honour and generosity, " that it was a man who *hated* him who thus dared to confide this sacred deposit to his care,"—in less dazzled moments, when the pageantries of the "Field of the Cloth of Gold" were not in action upon his chivalric feelings, fail of adding to his alarm of future evil.

The domestic calamity in the loss of his first-born, his embassy to Rome, and the subsequent distress of mind, interfered with Lord Harcourt's meditations upon the imprudent promise which he had been excited into making; and at length, when other causes led him into adopting his desultory movements during his first year of mourning for his wife, he almost hoped every clue to him might be lost, until time pressing for the education of the mysterious orphan might induce his protector to make some other arrangement for his asylum. But in this expectation his lordship was disappointed; for, in an obscure village in Normandy, whilst he was resting himself, horses, and suite, on his way to England, his mysterious *protégée* was presented to him for a page, by a monk of most prepossessing manners, whom Lord Harcourt found had been preceptor to his young charge whilst on travel through various countries for the last three years.

This most pleasing and enlightened monk informed Lord Harcourt privately, that the name by which he was to know his young page was Augustus Fitzwalter; and that this interesting and promising youth believed himself to be the offspring of parents then in voluntary banishment—a sort of exile not uncommon at this period. And most interesting and promising, Lord Harcourt soon pronounced Augustus: nor was the youth's prompt passport to favourable impression in a strikingly fine exterior a false light, that emanated lustre to deceive; for the heart and mind of Augustus were full as perfect works of Nature as his form and face. Many months had not elapsed, after his establishment in the family of his new patron, ere Fitzwalter became high in favour of every one connected with it.

At this period every noble could boast many places of residence; to each of which they usually migrated for some period every year. Lord Harcourt recoiling from the idea of ever beholding his Yorkshire castle more, determined to make Vespasian Tower his chief abode. Father Hubert was directed to superintend the education of Lord de Mandevillle and Augustus; whilst, as to Lady Louise, her father's own early prejudices led him to attend to those also of Lord Darlington, and the insidious remarks and representations of the designing Isabel: consequently, this poor child was, by general vote, deemed not moveable, but left in exile at Alba, with her attached governess, Maud, and a few of the old adherents and domestics, who all, from Lady Louise to the most ancient of the household, felt as if a precious blessing had been cruelly wrested from them when the unwelcome mandate bereaved them of Father Hubert, who, on his part, was overwhelmed with sorrow at parting from his earthly idol, Louise, for whom his heart cherished all the paternal affection he had borne her mother; and, with solemn and affecting exhortations, gave the child into the charge Father Jonathan, his successor at Alba.

Unfortunately for Lady Louise Father Jonathan was so devoted to

iterature that he considered nothing else worth existing for; and,
ully satisfied with his own capabilities, he had determined to astonish
he world with a learned work, to aid and illustrate the labours of
Martin Luther; and was anxiously engaged thereon when the unwelcome appointment assailed him, of preceptor to Louise. Like vital
drops from his heart's stream of life was the sacrifice of each moment
he was necessarily compelled to waste upon his pupil; and the rapidly
declining health of her governess exonerated him more and more from
he annoying task of teaching the young idea how to shoot.

Shortly after the death of the governess was known at Vespasian
Tower, a successor, selected by the Abbess of St. Mildred's, was appointed to supply the place of the deceased; but this successor became
almost immediately the avowed detestation of her pupil, who resolutely
recoiled from every acquirement to be obtained through the medium of
her new governante, except proficiency in burlesque mimicry, for which
the singularities and awkward defects of Dame Vintry, afforded ample
scope.

But not thus was the procedure of education in Vespasian Tower;
for there, through the good Hubert, were established all things which
could embellish the mind and manners of youth. Here was also to be

found, as in the earlier ages, every exercise for the promotion of chivalrous accomplishments, as well as every instruction in more modern literature.

Under the guidance of Lord Darlington, the new Lady Harcourt was contesting her daughter's claims to the title and estates of her progenitors; and the universal belief that these claims would be allowed, aiding the beauty and seductive manners of Marion Fitzstephen, yielded to her such importance in every circle, that no wonder romantic gallantry, encouraged by chivalrous education, led the youths assembled in Vespasian Tower very early to pronounce the peerless Marion the arbitress of their future fate. Amongst this number Marion early felt an anxious desire to enrol the captivating page, Augustus Fitzwalter; and often, more especially as time advanced, Lord Darlington feared his plan of waiting for his baroness was doomed to be subverted by the interloping *protégé* of Lord Harcourt.

Business, which could not be evaded, at length compelled Lord Harcourt to visit Alba; and as a companion, who would interest without annoying him with the trouble of ceremony, selected Augustus to accompany him into Yorkshire. With trembling fear Isabel saw her lord set out on this journey, anticipating that parental feelings might awaken interest for the hateful Louise, to the subversion of her plans, should her agents not have toiled effectually in preparing a blight for every germ of affection that otherwise might blossom into love for Louise.

As Lord Harcourt, his *protege*, and attendants entered upon the domain of Alba, Augustus, riding by his lordship's side, suddenly began to look around with great earnestness, and at length exclaimed—

" I think I have travelled this way, my lord, ere this."

" Have you?" responded his lordship, aroused by the exclamation from painful retrospections.

" Indeed have I, with my dear and good father Ulric, before we travelled abroad. But my revered preceptor gave no information, whatever was his motive, of the name of the country through which we travelled; I was not aware, therefore, of ever having been in Yorkshire."

" What object has your recognition found to give you assurance of this fact?" demanded Lord Harcourt.

" The yet remaining ruin of yon cot. At the moment it was fired father Ulric providentially made his approach, wending his way to a monastery, where we were to tarry for t he ;

" He was in time to be useful, then?"

" Some parent must soon have been childless by the flames, had he not happened to be at hand," responded Augustus. " There was the baptism of a bell at some monastery near; to which the attendants of two children had repaired, with many others, to witness the ceremony, leaving the poor babes without protection in yon cot. Whether through design or accident, a fire soon kindled amid the rushes, where the poor children had been left sleeping on the floor. At this moment of peril Father Ulric approached, and, attracted by the smoke, he sped to give assistance. Piteous cries soon gave wings to his motion. The door of the hut defied his strength, yet through its chasms issued volumes of smoke and flame. Ulric perceived a window, which he burst in; but, being too small for his body, I was the implement he found apt for his purpose. On my entrance, I found myself in a chamber adjoining that in flames, with no other outlet but the window I had entered and a door which was on fire, through which I beheld two children; one of whom, an infant, lay sleeping tranquilly upon a sack, which the other bantling, although not much more than a year older was, with all her baby might, dragging in wild affright from the pursuing flames, and, as it seemed, to sure destruction, yet, through the intuition of Providence, to the only spot in which its fate could have been avoided; and even in these moments of exertion, the affectionate little heroine was bending her own fairy form over her more helpless and unconscious brother to guard him from the flames. The poor babes were rescued from their fate, but the little heroine firmly lisped her refusal to tell aught that might enlighten us, since those who had left them had made dreadful threats against her brother, if she mentioned their absence to any one. We had, therefore, no other course but to follow the guidance of our ears, which soon led us, by the sounding of a convent bell, to a monastery of venerable structure; where, when we produced our bantlings, the utmost consternation was awakened, and the children were received with glad feelings by the nuns, but they obstinately refused to inform us to whom the babes belonged."

At this moment, and before Lord Harcourt could utter any comment upon Augustus' communication, a female child, shabbily attired, darted through a gap in the stone boundary of the road which our travellers were slowly pacing, and, heedless of danger, rushed to their horses' heads, and in tones of melting supplication " implored alms for a sick sufferer, who was perishing for lack of food." Although there was nothing strikingly attractive in the appearance of the young mendicant, yet the energy of her manner, and the pathos of her musical voice, drew forth a favourable response to her petition, from the purses of the travellers, when a flash of joy irradiated her countenance to almost celestial beauty; and, uttering a short but affecting burst of gratitude, she darted back through the aperture which she had emerged from, and with the speed of a lapwing pursued her way up a rising ground.

" Gramercy !" exclaimed the page, raising himself in his stirrups, to obtain a better view of the runaway; " Look, my lord, how graceful the urchin is, who, at first view, seemed so homely. She lacks no shape-smith : never did I observe one whose form and movements were more light and graceful."

" She is, indeed, a graceful zephyr," said Lord Harcourt; and marvellously apt for her mendicity, for the silvery tones of her supplicating voice went home to the heart, and left no doubt on the mind that urgent necessity impelled her solicitations. She is no common beggar."

The travellers shortly after reached the portal of Alba Castle, where, after sounding a loud peal, the gates slowly creaked in response, and the porter, upon beholding who demanded entrance, rapidly lowered the draw-bridge; and, whilst his cheeks blanched, and his lips quivered, he attempted to articulate a cheerful welcome to his unexpected lord.

Lord Harcourt's heart was too full of the memory of Adela at this moment to admit of more than a gracious wave of the hand, in recognition of the poor jester Littlewit; and the moment he entered the base-court, and had dismounted from his horse, he darted along the cloister which led to the chapel, leaving his valet to perform the honours to Augustus, who was speedily ushered into the castle, where the desolation of non-residence, which saddened this noble structure, with the solemn echo of the footfalls which now broke the melancholy silence, struck our page with the inhospitable chill of depopulation.

His lordship having private reasons for not apprising the Alba household of his coming, had dispatched no *avant-courier* to announce it: the consternation, therefore, with the novelty of action now spread by Littlewit, were indeed animating; and painfully so to Father Nicoli, who, through the absence of Father Jonathan, was called to the foreground in the reception of his lord. By an accidental detention on the road of an express from Isabel, the Abbess of St. Mildred was deprived of instructions how to act; and her agents in the castle, of intimation that would have spared them much embarrassment. However, this visit of Lord Harcourt to the chapel seemed to yield comfort to the disconcerted priest, in its promise of time for certain arrangements relative to Lady Louise, and which he instantly sought to accomplish. Through the absence of Father Ralph, with the personal preparation which sent all others to their duty, poor Littlewit was the only servant in attendance when his lordship at length emerged from the chapel, and entered the hall.

"What! Master Jester, have your wits left you?" said his lordship, endeavouring to exert his firmness: "what ails thee, that you lack all merry conceits to greet me with? Come, sparkle up, and yield me a jest withal."

"A sorry jester is a jest in sooth."

"Your wit has not improved by keeping, I perceive," returned his lordship, languidly.

"Not by keeping *silent*," retorted the jester: mine has been pent in so long, it has lost its edge; but should a *mute* be in request, heaven knows my fitness for the same."

"But, Sir Jester," said Augustus, hastily, perceiving the last reply struck harshly upon the feelings of Lord Harcourt, "where is the Lady Louise?"

"The Lady Louise! youth? Ask her gaolers," returned poor Littlewit, with strong emotion.

"What's this you say?" demanded Lord Harcourt, in surprise.

"God help me! I know not what may betide me if I turn babbler: Dame Vintry may abuse me, and the head of our church may excommunicate me ; yet, I stand the hazard," replied the jester, who was a sorry one indeed. "They know not how to manage Lady Louse, or they would find no trouble ; for she is a blossom of great promise, when gentle winds blow on her ; but when the blast comes harshly and fiercely, the tender shoot becomes a sturdy oak, unbending in the hurricane ; and when her lofty spirit leads her to resistance, the spiteful abbey-lubbers reverse their climax in severity and descent, to make superlative their punishment."

" Descent !"

" Ay, my lord, e'en below the level of the castle keep !"

The fine eyes of Lord Harcout flashed indignant ire, whilst his heart felt the first throb of paternal affection it had ever experienced for poor Louise ; and, loudly shouting for the seneschal, he was flying from the hall to seek his child, when he encountered Father Nicoli. · Instantly his lordship changed his tone, from parental feeling to that of politic dissembling, and, bestowing something like gracious recognition upon the evidently agitated Nicoli, demanded to see the Lady Louise.

" Dame Vintry is gone to prepare her young charge to receive the paternal blessing, and will then bring the Lady Louise hither," replied the trembling Nicoli.

" That cannot take long, and must have come to an end ere I can reach my child's chambers. I will, therefore, proceed there without delay. Lead on, good father."

The good father could not lead, for he could scarcely stand through agitation ; and with difficulty articulated—

" I am sorry, my lord, that upon Father Jonathan being summoned to attend a chapter"——

" A chapter of his own composition," muttered the jester.

" A chapter at York," continued Nicoli,—" the task fell to my lot, and a glad task I thought to find it, the guidance of our young frisking lamb in soberness to the good shepherd. But one word in privacy, my lord—well may your lordship tremble, for so do I—the diabolical damsel Maud, I soon discovered, had turned the hapless child from the true faith ; and she impiously declared she would not homage the sacred representations of our Holy Saints. My good lord, as we were bound in duty, we made every effort to save her from heresy ; but vain was every exertion whilst the tempter remained ; we therefore sent the serpent hence, in the form of the damsel Maud."

" What !" exclaimed his lordship, sternly ; " send the faithful Maud from Alba, without my consent !"

" It was our bounden duty, good my lord, albeit it proved of little avail. No gentleness could lure back the young apostate. Therefore it became us—yet with sorrowing hearts we do so—it became us just to place her—not, my good lord, for any long period, but only that it might recal her to the true faith—it behoved us, I say, good my lord to—to—place the Lady Louise—just in the first chamber—below—, below the keep. But to lead back the Lady Louise, to the path she had strayed from, was not our good fortune ; for even alone, with all the gloom of loneliness around her, she formed a plan to retaliate upon us. We gave no heed to the fact of the spiricles of the enclosure being formed to exclude the egress of grown captives only, and bethought us not that, as our jester says, the Lady Louise's form is so subtile, it can, when she likes, glide through key-holes, and though one of these spiricles she has made her escape."

The life's blood of Lord Harcourt seemed now to flow back from his heart with a sudden chill which almost froze the current through his veins; and staggering a few paces, he was caught and supported by Augustus and Littlewit; but was at length revived by a powerful cordial, when he eagerly exclaimed:—

"My child is safe from the perils of her escape!—For, despite her disguise, I recognise her. Yes! it was Adela's tones that struck to the heart of her unconscious father. But, Littlewit, tell me—for I am prepared to hear you assisted her to escape, and supplied her disguise, for whom was she under the degrading need of imploring alms?"

"For Maud," responded Littlewit. "Maud is famishing, and none but the Lady Louise would dare to give her assistance."

"Lead me to the habitation of poor ill-requited Maud," exclaimed Harcourt, in evident agitation: and catching the arm of Father Nicoli, to stay him, continued—Hold, sir! I prohibit your anticipation of my visit there. Seneschal! neither do you quit my sight; you must be content to walk with me to Maud's residence, with Littlewit for our guide. Augustus, your arm. I prophesy, we shall soon learn how your charitable donation has been disposed of."

In moody silence the party proceeded to the very ruins which Augustus had pointed out; and not more evident agitation did the anxious father evince on this walk than the monk betrayed, for he shook perceptibly. When they arrived at the wretched hovel, Littlewit addressed his lord.

"This miserable dwelling is that of the faithful Maude. Through the breaches made by fire in the walls, my lord may behold his daughter."

"These breaches presented to the vision of the agitated parent, and his young friend, a miserable pallet of rushes on the mud floor within, upon which a human form lay extended, and by whom the youthful mendicant was kneeling, in the act of arranging the sack of chaff which served for poor Maud's pillow. The ejaculation of horror which escaped his lordship's lips, on his first glance into the sick chamber of Adela's faithful and favourite attendant, aroused the startled and tender nurse of poor Maud to her feet, when, through the chasms in the wall perceiving Father Nicoli, Louise wildly shrieked as she threw herself across the pallet, and grasping Maud with all her might, exclaimed—

"He shall not tear me from you, Maudy!"

"Fear not, Louise," said his lordship, mildly, as he now entered the hovel; when Louise, upon seeing him whom she had just received kindness from, conceiving, that, although accompanied thither by the stern Father Nicoli, he was not likely to have come to harm her, started up to implore further assistance from the benevolent stranger for the comforts of poor Maude, and in that instant she was clasped to the bosom of him she was about to supplicate.

"Louise," said Lord Harcourt, tenderly,; "Louise, does no internal feeling whisper that I am your father?"

Lord Harcourt felt, as he held his daughter in his arms, the electricity conveyed by this question through the frame of the sensitive Louise, upon whose surprise, joy, hope, and fear so powerfully operated that in less than a moment the alarmed father found his child had fainted in his arms.

The consternation was excessive, as this miserable ruin afforded no restorative, save the pure stream that purled past the door; but this simple remedy proved efficacious. Louise's unclosed eyes that were no longer invisible, smiled up at her father, burst into tears, and then hid her head upon his bosom. But a painful recollection soon recalled her from this indulgent anxiety for poor Maud, like an undulating breeze turning the ivy's straying tendril from the oak it was entwining, to rest upon some intervening bough; and softly Louise whispered her earnest petition for the rescue of Maud from persecution.

"Maude shall be removed to her home at Alba, where you shall be her only nurse, Louise," said his lordship; and then turning to Maude, kindly inquired how she came in this woeful plight.

Maud's tale was short, but piteous. She had been first turned into a wanderer from the castle, then from the charitable roof that had sheltered her, through threats of ecclesiastic vengeance; and when a cold, caught in a hovel's ruin, in which she had been driven to seek a shelter, deprived her of the power of longer working for her bread, she must must have perished for lack of food, only for Littlewit, who brought some daily to her. But even of this relief the malignant monks had for the last two days deprived her, and she was gradually sinking to eternal rest, when, late the preceding evening, her fleeting spirit had been recalled to sensibility by the tears and caresses of the Lady Louise, who had sat on the ground weeping by her all the night; and, after a short disappearance, had brought her food, despite every denunciation.

During the latter part of Maud's narrative, uttered in the tremulous tones of pitiable weakness, the cheeks of Louise were mantled by the brightest blushes of modest sensibility, pained at hearing her own praises; and at length she endeavoured to hide her glowing face upon the bosom of her father, who demanded, in a tone of kindness—

"Where she had obtained the food?"

"I dare not tell you," she softly replied; "the monk would be so filled with vengeance against the kind dame I coaxed the pottage from, and who is gone to a druggist's for me, to bring me balms to do my Maudy good. But it was your kindness that bought the mess I brought for Mand."

Lord Harcourt now gave orders to the seneschal and Littlewit to repair to the castle for a comfortable litter for the conveyance of Maud;

" and while we are waiting the arrival of this conveyance," continued his lordship, " this dear child will, I trust, recover her surprise, and be able, with your support, Master Augustus, to walk to the castle."

Louise, starting, turned with eager scrutiny to observe the page, when, after a momentary investigation, she turned away with a look of disappointment.

" Why, Louise, would you not betray the names of those who advise you not to homage graven images?" demanded Lord Harcourt. " By such an avowal you might have saved Maud and yourself the evils you have each endured."

" I did state," responded Louise, " that it was Father Jonathan ; but," and she blushed to the brightest vermilion of indignation, " they were as mindless of Louise's word as if she were a churl's brat ; and sent my poor Maudy into the world, to make me weep."

" But you did not weep," said Father Nicoli, with bitterness : " tears would have beseemed contrition. No, in despite of her birth, the Lady Louisa was changed into a fury."

" Was such your conduct, Louise ?" inquired his lordship.

" Indeed it was," returned Louisa, blushing again. " They dragged Maudy from my grasp, though I implored them piteously not to take her away, the fury came into me, all boiling up ; and as it chafed my swelling heart, it made me strong and desperate, and I called them base names, and mocked them."

Lady Louisa now, as a climax to her ingenuousness, performed the distortion of her face into the similitude of that of Father Nicoli ; but although a caricature, yet so ludicrously resembling him, that none could remain in doubt of the original, and so nearly did she overthrow the gravity of her father by her comic powers that with difficulty he preserved his composure. But not so successful was poor Augustus, for, in defiance of every feeling of respect for the sacred function, he laughed outright ; nor could he call his risible faculties to order, even though tears trickled, as it seemed in penitence, down his dimpled cheeks. Father Nicoli marked all this, and never forgave Fitzwalter.

At length the litter arrived : poor Maud was tenderly placed in it, and borne away towards Alba, followed by Father Nicoli in high dudgeon, Lord Harcourt, Augustus, and the delighted Lady Louise.

On the way to the castle it was necessary to cross that brook where, some years back, Maud had encountered the gay St. Aubin. The tide was now at the ebb, and stepping-stones made a pass for pedestrians. The litter was borne safely across ; and Father Nicoli pacing immediately after, in the carelessness of action which his moodiness inspired, slipped off the stones into the water. Lord Harcourt and Fitzwalter, possibly through contempt of the man from his inhumanity, had not been particularly alert in springing forward to afford assistance : however that might be, the little Louise had preceded them, and caught his hand with the kind intent to aid him, exclaiming, in a tone of soft compassion—

"Oh, poor Father Nicoli!"

But Father Nicoli flung her hand from him as he recovered his equilibrium, and his footing on the stones. Lord Harcourt seized up his child in his arms, and pressed her to his bosom with parental exultation; and, after a moment of excited sensibility, addressed Father Nicoli with a smile—

"Have we not conviction now, holy father, that the faith of this child is, without disguise, purely Christian?"

Father Nicoli's cheeks blanched, and he made no reply; for the spirit within him, which worshipped Mammon, whispered that he had

injured his own interest by punishing the Lady Louise for heresy, since he now perceived the noxious germ had proceeded from the parent stock. Full of this discovery, he panted to reach St. Mildred's, there to spread the alarm, and to consult upon the measures which might be decreed for adoption. The arrival of the party at Alba procured his liberation, and Father Nicoli lost not a moment in visiting St. Mildred's. At length he returned to the castle, fully instructed to bend and bow to Lord Harcourt, and in all things to deceive him.

CHAPTER XII.

It was a mournful necessity for Lord Harcourt to go over the castle with the seneschal, to arrange for requisite repairs; but, in his now frequent perambulations through the sombre premises, he found the little Louise continually crossing his path with some wild or hoyden prank, which often shocked his courtly manners, yet frequently excited his risibility; until at length he pronounced her a most enlivening appendage to the castle.

But, unluckily for Louise, his lordship's devotedness to exterior embellishments wofully impeded her way to the full paternal tenderness of his heart. She had awakened unqualified approbation for the excellence of disposition which she had evinced on the first day of his arrival, so powerfully, that had she possessed even half the personal beauty which he required to ornament his offspring, he would have taken her to his heart's core at once.

A few days after his lordship's arrival at Alba, wishing to make personal inquiries for some of the tenantry upon the domain, he sallied forth, accompanied by Augustus. Louise, unobserved and uninvited, scampered after them. Ere aware of being so accompanied, Lord Harcourt perceiving a cottager at some distance in advance, whom he thought he recognised, shouted after the man, but without effect, for the poor rustic was impenetrably deaf. Again and again his lordship shouted, and so did Augustus, but still in vain—when suddenly a yell assailed their ears, issuing from behind them, so shrill, so discordant, so out of Nature's class of tones, and so terrific, that Lord Harcourt, a man of dauntless courage, rushed forward to escape the pending danger; no wonder, then, the youthful page awaited no second call to fly with him.

On they scudded until nearly breathless, when his lordship's intrepidity rallied, from having escaped the onslaught from the wild animal they fled from, and he faced about to reconnoitre what sort of form the creature wore, when the only living object which met his eager scrutiny was the fleet Louise, scampering towards him.

His lordship, alarmed at her peril, rushed back, and snatching his child up into his arms, fled to the tree into which Augustus had by this time climbed for refuge, from what he conceived no common source of alarm.

Scarcely had this trio obtained firm establishment in their widely spreading sanctuary, and Lord Harcourt ejaculated a fervent thanksgiving for their deliverance from this beast of prey, when the alarmed page demanded from Lady Louise, who was in high delight at this unexpected elevation, " If she had seen the animal that had yelled so dreadfully?"

"It was I who yelled," returned Louise, calmly. "But what was it frightened you?"

"Why, Lady Louise did—if Lady Louise shouted forth that yell of yells," replied Augustus, half laughing at the possibility, yet half incredulous—

"You are only jesting, for you assert an impossibility, child," exclaimed his lordship.

"'Tis true, nevertheless; and what moved me to do so was, I thought your courtly voice was not likely to reach the hearing of old Beetlehead."

"But how could you utter tones so unfeminine, unnatural, and terrific, child?" demanded his lordship, fretfully.

"Why, it is the very way that Bellowbear always shouts to poor Beetlehead; and he alone can make the old man hear. But, Lady Louise, it is not meet for you, a female of high estate, to imitate the the masculine discordance of an uncouth clown."

"I know the squalling was unseemly, for it made my own flesh to creep to hear its din," returned Louise, meekly, looking down abashed; "but it was the only means to effect the desired object, my lord."

"I thank you, Louise; but must prevent such unbecoming articulations in future," said his lordship as he commenced his descent from the tree, in no very amicable humour with poor Louise. Before his lordship's feet had touched the ground, or Augustus moved to the point which he conceived most convenient for passing Lady Louise into her father's receiving arms, that volatile spirit had evaporated from the tree and escaped his aid, by swinging down upon a lower branch, and from thence dropping himself unhurt by the side of the astonished peer.

"From these antics," exclaimed his lordship, half alarmed and half annoyed, yet almost inclining to risibility, "we must give credence to some monkey having purloined from Alba the true Lady Louise, leaving me one of its own active offspring in her stead. What think you, Augustus?"

"Augustus! Augustus!" repeated Louise, thoughtfully, as she now walked onward with the page. "I wish I knew where to find another kindly boy Augustus—not so big by half as this one, and with somewhat less curling hair."

"Why, where have you encountered such an Augustus?" demanded Fitzwalter eagerly. "It seemeth to me that I once saw Lady Louise, when she was not half so big as she now is. And to let her into a secret, I was once an Augustus not half so big as I now am, and then had hair too short for curling."

"Then it was you—you, your own very self, that saved my darling brother from being burnt alive!" exclaimed Louise, in a tone of ecstatic joy, as she fled back to her father, shouting audibly; but the tones, being her own natural ones, were thrillingly melodious. "My lord! my honoured father! this Master Augustus it was who so aptly repaired to the assistance of my baby brother, and saved him from the flames!" and Louise, having made this announcement burst into tears.

THE WITCHES' CLIFF; OR,

Lord Harcourt, who had loitered behind his companion to meditate upon the possible causes of this rough gem having received so little polish from those instructors whom he had been led to believe fully competent to the task assigned to them, now caught the extended hands of the agitated Louise, whose tears of gratitude taught his own to start to his eyes ; and, turning from her, he clasped in his expanding arms the preserver of his children.

Augustus received the ebullitions of his lordship's gratitude with modest grace ; though shrinking in apprehension that it might appear he had been conscious whose children he had been the instrument of saving from destruction, when he had mentioned the circumstance to Lord Harcourt ; or, at least, that it had not been inadvertently, his aiding the awakening recognition of Lady Louise.

" But how came you to be encountered with such peril, Louise ?" demanded Augustus, anxious to escape from his lord's oppressive gratitude.

" I have no accurate recollection of it," returned Louise ; " for it was ere my darling, the last of all my kindred, was taken from me. It was when Maudy was close pent up in tending old Dame Bostock, who was seriously ill. So the dear baby Edward's foster-mother, and his nursery maids, took me as a playfellow for Edward while they went out ; but I know not why they left us in that dark hovel, where a grim old woman sat in the middle on the hearth, breaking sticks and firing them ; and when the baby cried himself to sleep, the old woman told me not to stir if I valued my brother's life, and then went her way. So I stirred not until the rushes on the floor were in a blaze : then I shrieked in affright, and the good little boy Augustus, like a succouring angel, flew in at the window to our aid, and snatched the sweet baby from the flames."

" How is this, Louise," said his lordship, " that all your gratitude to Fitzwalter makes it lavished upon the preserver of your brother ; whilst the fact of his having saved your own life seems totally forgotten ?"

Louise started, blushed, and frankly acknowledged she had never once thought of her individual obligation.

Lord Harcourt, with a smile, inquired from the preserver of his children whether he thought this extraordinary omission in Lady Louise's recollection proceeded from a flaw in the perceptions of her gratitude, or was caused by the acuteness of affection for her brother monopolising every thought from self?

The interesting page was firmly convinced there existed no flaw in the sensibilities of Lady Louise ; and such being also the opinion of Lord Harcourt, his lordship sighed in anticipating apprehension for her future happiness, when such enthusiasm in susceptibility should be combined with an exterior little likely to elicit any reciprocity, at least in the most tender sympathy of the heart.

Louise had now taken such hold upon her father's interest, that she often formed the theme of his discourse with his young companion

Augustus; and his lamentation was frequent upon the striking and unfortunate contrast she exhibited, in attractive graces, to Isabel and her daughter.

Although Isabel's ingratitude to her benefactress had wakened Lord Harcourt's estimation of her moral excellence almost to an overthrow, his belief of her intellectual pre-eminence was unimpaired; and his infatuated attachment being still unsubdued, though not in the idolatrous climax it once had soared to, he firmly credited all her statements relative to those in whom his daughter's education had been confided: nor did his interviews with the Abbess of St. Mildred's upon this important subject promise any thing auspicious for poor Louise; for the wily abbess assured his lordship that Lady Louise's intractability could not be subdued; and that Dame Vintry was fully equal to the embellishing a second Isabel, had nature here presented her with such a docile being for her tuition.

It was after a long conference with this wily abbess, upon the forlorn hope of his volatile child's improvement, that Lord Harcourt, on re-entering his castle, encountered the wild Louise, sporting her way down a staircase, with no very graceful show of that comic buffoonery her buoyancy of animal spirits just then inspired.

His lordship, being in no very placid humour with his daughter (for the statements of the abbess were in full operation), exclaimed, as sternly as the not yet extinct feeling of chivalric courtesy would permit towards a female—

"Is such the seemly method, Louise, for a young lady to make descent of a staircase?"

"Indeed, I know not," responded Louise, smiling; "for I never saw a lady go up or down stairs since I was of age to notice it."

This innocent, unconscious reproof for the method of her rearing went promptly to her father's conscience; as the tones of sweetness in which it was uttered thrilled to his heart, with conviction, that in fascination of voice in speaking this wild plant infinitely surpassed both Isabel and her daughter; and while these dulcet tones vibrated through his parental feelings, something kindly whispered, "surely nature never left such melody unaccompanied: and there must be other harmonies within, could we but strike their sounding:" and from this suggestion his lordship demanded an immediate interview with Mrs. Vintry, who had hitherto evaded meeting him, to form his own judgment, if possible, upon whom the fault rested of the unrefined bearings of his daughter.

Fortunately for poor Lady Louise, Mrs. Vintry was strikingly hideous; had clumsy red hands, which were intrusively conspicuous, through the awkward mismanagement of these unruly members; and had in her articulation a sort of lisp, which, combined with plebeian diction, and the then almost unintelligible pronunciation of the rustics of Yorkshire, gave to her elocution a degree of barbarism from which the ear of refinement could not but recoil: therefore, upon achieving one glance at her deformities, and hearing one speech of her oratory, his lordship felt conviction of the total incapacity of this blur in nature for the preceptress of his daughter; and, in amazement at how the talented abbess of St. Mildred's could in possibility have been infatuated into a contrary opinion, determined to dispel the magic which must be in operation upon her judgment, by his absolute decree against this woman; and to request the abbess to seek a competent successor to this uncouth animal, such as her own judgment and refinements could approve.

The business which had brought Lord. Harcourt to Alba being at length arranged, the hour of his departure drew near; and Father Jonathan, having returned to the castle, was solemnly invested by his lordship with the sole care of Lady Louise's religious principles; and a mandate as solemnly issued that Father Nicoli was never more to hold jurisdiction over her.

The day arrived in which Lord Harcourt and his little suite were to set out for Kent, and Louise was permitted to join the breakfast party of her father: but sorrow was her banquet; and at length, overshadowing her pale and pensive face with both her hands, she sobbed in silent grief. The hands which the little Louise gave thus to full view were beautifully formed; the tears, therefore, which trickled through her taper fingers penetrated to a chord of tender sympathy in her father's bosom; and when at length he was compelled to leave his insulated child, and in the care of those with whom he was not satisfied, her burst of artless affliction, sounding in the soft and touching tones of the heart's sore anguish, filled his breast with tender parental feelings.

CHAPTER XIII.

THROUGH close attendance upon his sovereign in the gay scenes devised at this period by Sir Thomas Wyatte, as well as by the wily management of the invidious Isabel, Lord Harcourt was gradually losing those lively impressions of parental tenderness for his forlorn child which her artlessness and affectionate sensibility had inspired; when a singular coincidence occurred, in his lordship receiving, at almost the same moment, a letter from Isabel's daughter, and one from Lady Louise; and a more striking contrast could scarcely have been arranged by the most ingenious contriver, than these compositions exhibited. Marion was at this period with the Worlingtons in Paris; consequently, her epistle was from thence; and it was written with mathematical parallelism; every line betraying her mental acquisitions, the admiration she excited, or the plaudits she had elicited from her various instructors.

Louise's achievement was written in the straggling varieties of serpentine meandering, in all sized characters, and diversified with blots of conspicuous opacity; the subject, chiefly assurances that she had paid strict attention to all her father's orders, manifold and puzzling as they were.

"In proof," said Lady Louise, "though full of affright at the unapt management of my pen, I obey your behest, my honoured lord and father, by my writing as soon as Father Jonathan has allowed me. He has told me to begin my rude letter with my heart's love to my good father. I am burning with impatience to tell you that I have done with my lackbrain tricks; that is, forsooth, a marvellous company of them. I no longer bite my lips, nor wink my eyelids, nor make mouths, nor writhe my forehead, nor frown, nor stare; and now, I never stand on one foot, while I spank the other to and fro, to rouse the dust and rushes. I am no longer noisy—I have ceased to lodge my elbows upon tables; I neither cough nor sneeze now at the break-fast board, albeit great may be my need. But, my lord, I still ride the roan jennet without saddle or housing, and tease and chafe him by tickling him with his own leash; for I cannot remember your having said nay to these gambols."

Lord Harcourt and Augustus Fitzwalter were in the apartments of Isabel when Lady Louise's epistle was delivered to his lordship; who, although shocked and conscience-stricken, could scarcely subdue symptoms of risibility at this artless egotism; which Lady Harcourt perceiving, she requested to be favoured with hearing read a perform-ance which seemed amusing.

During his lordship's compliance with this request, Isabel looked conscientiously shocked: and when he had ended, she exclaimed, with a sigh of compassionate regret—

"Alas! how unlike to Marion's!"

"Marion has been a fortunate girl, brought up with her mother; Louise a bereaved and neglected child," replied Lord Harcourt, in a tone of chagrin. "This epistle of poor Louise's is, it grieves me to say, not meet for her estate; yet there is much in the composition that yields me comfort. It seems to me to promise, that, if my daughter is not to become man's assassin, like yours, Isabel, she may prove his friend! Here, Augustus, make your own view of Lady Louise's letter, and tell me, albeit it is scant of method, may we not anticipate improvement in this artless child?"

Augustus, in approaching his lordship to receive the letter, perceived on the ground a second letter from Lady Louise, which had fallen un-observed by her father from the envelope, and bore the date of nearly a year after its companion: it was written much more steadily than its predecessor, and in its commencement she announced that the senes-chal had forgotten to send off her first letter—a matter that had not been discovered sooner.

"My honoured father," she wrote, "will be apt to imagine, by the miscarriage of my rude letter, that lack of memory is a disease in Alba Castle; but, in troth, mine has never failed since the good Augustus saved my life as well as my crother's, becomes each day more dear in my remembrance. Neither do I forget the visit of my father: no, indeed, since it was like the rising of the sun in spring after a drear winter, and, when it set, left rays behind still to warm the wild plant it shone upon. But I cannot imagine that the reckless memory which has departed from me has strayed to Edward; for I still hope he has not forgotten me; and knowing how well he wields his pen, he would not have ceased to glad me with his letters. I therefore think *you* have some "forgetful" seneschal at Vespasian Tower. Oh, my dear father, refresh his memory, and see that the long-looked for letters of my darling brother be sent to his loving sister; for in sooth, my father, as that bright sun which so saddened me when it went down the valley from Alba arose no more to shine on me, I do want something to cheer me."

Isabel, having failed in the intended effect of her insidious observation, was undecided upon the course she should pursue, effectively to obliterate the interest which Lady Louise's letter had awakened in the paternal bosom: his lordship, therefore. encountered nothing to abstract his anxious thoughts from his poor neglected child; and ere the day closed he despatched a packet to Alba, containing, besides an affectionate epistle and gifts from himself to Louise, a peremptory order to Father Jonathan for the immediate dismissal of Mrs. Vintry, whether a successor could be obtained or not—so much did apprehension of her uncouth diction and elocution being engrafted on his child alarm him. Nor did his lordship permit the departure of his messenger, without a long letter and presents for Louise from her brother, who assured his father that he had never suffered any opportunity to escape him of writing to his sister.

Augustus, too, retired from Lady Harcourt to write, and also about Lady Louise; and for many a year after, he remained unconscious that this epistle of his operated as the fate of Louise; and yet it was so.

Lord Harcourt was led to believe his mandate was about to be instantly obeyed, for Father Jonathan wrote him intimation that the Abbess of St. Mildred's had at length found a competent successor for Dame Vintry. His lordship's parental anxieties relative to Louise were thus consigned to rest; and, with his solicitude, his remembrance of her seemed to sink into a calm repose, from which his political employments ordained that he should not find leisure to awaken; for not a year now elapsed in which he did not spend the greater part in some continental embassy, defeating or aiding alternately the schemes of Charles, Francis, or the Roman See; but upon which excursions the beautiful Isabel had reasons for not accompanying him; and although the task was difficult, to withhold her society upon these occasions, without awakening suspicion or wounding Lord Harcourt's affection, she contrived her difficult manœuvring to her heart's content; and during these periods of her lord's absence she held her court with almost regal splendour at Vespasian Tower, the admiration of all whom the hospitality and magnificence of her revels allured to this beautiful domain.

Time thus advanced, until Edward Lord de Mandeville had entered his thirteenth, Augustus completed his eighteenth, and the pretty Marion advanced in her seventeenth, year.

Lord de Mandeville was indebted to nature for a most beautiful exterior, and many mental treasures ; and to Father Hubert de Bourg for as solid a store of intellectual advantages as a learned, pious, diligent, and anxious preceptor could enrich so very a youth with. But Lord de Mandeville was not the perfect being that good Father Hubert had toiled so sedulously to make him; for the often

injudicious lenity of his adoring father, and the pernicious indulgences of his designing stepmother, gave energy to his faults, amongst which obstinacy of resolution in serious matters was the most prominent ; whilst, in minor concerns, the whimsicalities of his caprices and the petulance of his froward humours were tormenting even to those who, knowing the excellence of his heart, sincerely loved him. These minor foibles had been augmented by no small degree of personal vanity, awakened by the unqualified admiration he excited, when, by the command of his sovereign, he performed, though scarcely six years old, one of the principal characters in the play enacted by children at Greenwich, when the ambassadors from Francis invested Henry with the order of St. Michael.

Augustus Fitzwalter, now arrived at the honour of 'squire in chivalry, was also indebted to nature for a strikingly fine and prepossessing exterior; even such as to awaken the prompt admiration, and fix the approving gaze, of every beholder. Nature, too, had enriched him with a heart wherein all of human excellence was centred; and an understanding equal to every attainment, both in solidity and embellishment. With courage the most dauntless, yet the dove of peace seemed the genial nestling of his bosom. Domestic life, the tenderness of parental love, the unity of affectionate brotherhood, were the sunbeams which his heart coveted; but these were not for him. Augustus was an isolated being, without one kindred tie to warm his heart, and knowing nothing relative to his family, but that they were honourable, unfortunate, voluntary exiles; and that his guardian himself, all mystery, had been called by his own ambiguous fate from Britain.

The premature perfections of Marion awakened no expectation, in the mind of sober reasoners, of improvement; for she had seemed to reach the climax of perfection in the moment of creation. But those who did not think upon the subject, perhaps, expected something even still more exquisite to dazzle admiration, as she expanded into maturity of form and understanding; and, probably, disappointment in this expectation might have operated to her disadvantage, had not art, her potent auxiliary, contrived for her a vestment of brilliant deception to conceal deficiencies. Marion's book of study was, "How to attract;" and every thought, wish, and action, were to promote that darling purpose. Nature and education having so eminently gifted her with every exterior grace and beauty, her toils were superfluous, when aimed to rivet the eye of admiration; but her mind being far from perfect, and possessing not one innate treasure of the heart, it had early become her project to establish counterfeit virtues that should pass for the genuine. All things, therefore, which were sweet, and gentle, and obliging, and forbearing, and friendly, and charitable, she personated sedulously. To the aged she was venerating—to the foolish, compassionate—to the sick, tender—to the faulty, lenient—to the indigent, charitable: and all this Marion performed most winningly, even without one drop of the sweet milk of human kindness in her composition; while, in the execution of her benevolence, she sustained no individual privations—for when, with well arranged display, she bore alms to the poor, the purse or buttery of Lord Harcourt supplied the dole. But yet, though thus accomplished for prowess against the heart of man, Marion was, at the then considered far advanced stage of spinsterism, seventeen—not only unmated, but without engagement.

But this disengaged state was not occasioned by lack of adorers; and she had absolutely only to name the elected, to make numbers wretched. Marion, therefore, with admirable dexterity, kept all her game in view, consigning none to despair.

Had Marion's heart been the sole agent in the disposal of her hand, Augustus Fitzwalter had probably been the elected; but, as ambition was the chief actuater in Marion's bosom, Augustus could not be chosen whilst mystery thus hung around his origin and estate. He was evidently an adorer of Marion, though a silent one—at least, silent upon the subject of his admiration.

Lord de Mandeville, despite his extreme youth, was another of these speculations Marion held in suspension, ready to swoop upon should ambition pronounce it expedient.

As to Lord Darlington, he still weakly cherished his romantic project for his espousal with his early captivator.

About the period when our young *dramatis personæ* had attained those ages just mentioned, the long pending decision upon the Fitzstephen succession was brought to a final hearing. Marion, through the interest awakened by the magic of her charms, more than through the unquestionable establishment of her legitimate right, was pronounced the lawful heir. She therefore assumed the title of Baroness Fitzstephen : but with estates so embarrassed—so taxed with forfeitures to the crown for the misdeeds of her progenitors—that her means of supporting her dignity were scarcely more than nominal.

Long ere the pending suit had terminated, Marion had, in the imprudence of castle-building hospitality, promised her young companions that they should accompany her when she took possession of Fitzstephen Castle ; where she would entertain them with pageants and revels of the most beautiful description. To rescind this promise without prejudice to her popularity, she deemed impossible ; and how to manage its performance, without betraying the barrenness of the soil that was to furnish the supplies, for a time puzzled her and her more experienced mother. At length Isabel formed a project worthy of her, which would throw the whole party bound for Fitzstephen Castle into that of Alba ; where they should remain at her now niggardly lord's sole expense, until she could work upon his generosity through some new stratagem, to permit their proceeding to their place of ostensible destination with desirable effect.

This project contained a second attraction for the designing Isabel ; for, in the absence of her lord, it would afford an opportunity for presenting Lady Louise to those whom she wished to recoil from her, in that garb of uncouth ignorance which she had toiled to consolidate for this object of her diabolic hatred.

Lord Harcourt was at this moment on a continental mission, from which there was no immediate prospect of his being released ; and the absence of Father Hubert from scenes where the daughter of his revered countess was to be exhibited as an object for derision and disgust was also important.

As soon as the excursion was arranged for Fitzstephen Castle, Isabel began, as it were, to anticipate the sarcastic remarks of Sir Lionel upon the discomforts awaiting the party in Marion's mansion.

At length the travelling vehicles—light waggons gaily trapped—set out, accompanied by a numerous cavalcade and attendants.

Lord de Mandeville felt disconcerted, on perceiving himself of little consequence where Marion reigned sole paramount.

All the party had evinced unusually wild spirits during the journey ; and when they adjourned to the hostel for the night, Isabel, as if influenced by a sudden ebullition of this whole day's exuberant vivacity, proposed the frolic of surprising the unsophisticated Lady Louise, and the drones of Alba, by an unexpected visit, as the sovereign, consort, and court, on a progress.

The thoughtless Edward gladly seconded the motion, because he believed that in his father's castle he must be deemed a personage of consequence ; and Sir Lionel gave it his firm support, since he felt assured the adoption of the frolic must afford him ample scope for satire. But Augustus Fitzwalter, who was just returned from Paris, whither he had accompanied the Duke of Richmond and Lord Surrey two years prior, to study at the university there, could not approve the measure ; because he felt it unfair, if not cruel, to poor Lady Louise, who must, he feared, be scarcely equal to receive the party as they stood in their own individual rank, even had she and the castle household been prepared for their reception : but for such a host to come unexpectedly upon her, as her sovereign and court, in a dwelling despoiled, by non-residence, not only of every household adornment, but of absolute necessaries, was, he considered, more than common humanity could justify ; and he therefore toiled to counteract their sportive cruelty.

No sooner was this long mentally arranged, though suddenly announced, proposition of Lady Harcourt acceded to, than all who were to be engaged in the performance of it were appointed to the characters they were to personate in this masque of a royal progress. Lord Darlington, as king ; Lady Fitzstephen, the beautiful new consort, Jane Seymour ; Sir Lionel, as Sir Thomas Wyatte ; Augustus, as Duke of Richmond ; &c.

CHAPTER XIV.

THE imagination of the kind Augustus worked hard to befriend poor Louise, as the party of frolickers drew near to Alba Castle, without his having been able to turn them from their project. He felt, as a portentous cloud over his love-horoscope, the offending Lady Harcourt by circumventing her mirthful scheme ; yet he also felt that he should act unfaithfully to his lord, were he to allow a matter to take full effect, that would so keenly wound and mortify his parental pride and tenderness.

At length the fair star Marion and her satellites quartered for the night within a few miles of Alba : and scarcely were they assembled in the hostelry, ere they were most unexpectedly joined by Sir Rupert Fitzstephen, the late opponent of Marion for the honours of their ancestors. Sir Rupert was a genuine scion of the genealogical tree—a determined dauntless son of dissipation, with a fine exterior, a clear head, and a depraved heart. His fortunes through the late decree had become to the last extremity desperate ; and ere he should embrace the profession of a freebooter, the penal liabilities of which not promising much pleasure in perspective, he had followed his fair and fortunate opponent into Yorkshire, to develop how she might prove useful to him.

The hope of winning the royal influence upon the decree of his pending cause had led the vile Rupert to become one of the principal of the suborned witnesses, who had, in full career of perjury, given fatal testimony against the unfortunate and thoughtless Anne Boleyn ; and although the interest of the Seymours for Marion had operated against him in this speculation, yet still it was believed he was in high favour with his sovereign for this late nefarious service : his plausible excuses, therefore, for being in that auspicious spot so opportunely to greet his fair kinswoman, were received as the *very essence of veracity ; yet the courtesy of Isabel to Sir Rupert was accompanied by secret alarm.

This unexpected addition to the party only increased Augustus's anxiety to apprise Lady Louise of the approaching guests ; and ere he retired for the night, he, with a bright blush of shame for the trespass against veracity he was thus induced to commit, informed Lord Darlington of his intention to set out, ere dawn of day, to give the surprise of an unexpected visit to a friend, who was staying at a neighbouring monastery.

Having arranged for a pair of fleet horses and a trusty guide to be in readiness ere the day appeared, Augustus set off through all the intricacies and dangers of a shortened route to Alba ; and when at length he had arrived at a convenient station for his purpose, sent his guide, carefully schooled in the necessary caution of his mission, to summon Littlewit to a secret conference.

Augustus had not been long solus in his ambush, when a motley garb appeared in view. Promptly our young 'squire hailed the wearer, assured it must be the very motley he wished to see ; nor was he mistaken ; for in a moment he recognised Littlewit, little altered since they had met : but the striking change which had taken place in the boy, now sprouted into an adult, bewildered the recollection of the jester ; and Fitzwalter having promptly announced himself, inquired how fared the Lady Louise.

" Odd's pity ! I left the Lady Louise, good sir," responded Littlewit, "like to the grass beneath us here, bathed in pearly distillation. As usual, Master Augustus, when the seneschal replenishes the dear child's purse, anon the cash is gone ; and none can tell, by any cunning they possess, how the matter is managed. Having lately bought a strong box, guarded as craftily as might be invented, the dear child, in fancied security, made promise of a deed of charity, to be performed this very morning ; when, lo ! to her grief, and our astonishment, the cash again had vanished."

"This loss is untoward on many accounts," said Augustus; "but cannot you manage to replace it from my purse?"

"Nay, Sir 'Squire, the hawk is not more quick of sight than our young Louise. She would perhaps make discovery, like an astrologer, that the marks were not her own; and the spirit of the noble race she sprang from would chafe at the imposition."

"Present the promised gift even now," returned Augustus, impatiently, "for we must not allow grief now to afflict her; for she will soon have cause to exert her energies of mind; and although forbidden to mention it, I could not rest until I had apprised her of unexpected illustrious guests, even now in progress hither."

"Beshrew them! Not the court in progress, I trust," exclaimed Littlewit; "for then our dear Lady Louise would soon become a decapitated seraph to bedeck the tomb of poor Anne Boleyn."

"Your meaning, good Master Jester?"

"Why, Sir 'Squire, our neighbour, the new Lord Abbott of St. Stephen's, presented to our Lady Louise, as the gift of an unnamed friend of hers, a fairy book of devotion, written upon vellum, and in a cover of solid gold, with a ring to append it to the neck-chain or girdle; and being advised Queen Anne was apt to make presents of such, and that Bishop Latimer was in correspondence with this abbot, it struck us that the Queen was the secret sender of this gift. Thus gratitude to Queen Anne has found its way to the heart of Lady Louise and she sorely grieved for the sad fate of the martyred lady. Lady Louise not having yet learned to disguise her honest feelings, I fear the king's visit to Alba may endanger our dear child's safety.

"But, Littlewit, you must caution Lady Louise upon her behaviour, and represent the hazard of incautious remarks."

"Well! Sir 'Squire, as the gratitude of our youthful lady to you has never slumbered, I will communicate your advice to her; and then, perchance, she may take a more prudent view of the matter."

"Lady Louise must not know of my performing herald," exclaimed Augustus in alarm, "lest, in her ingenuousness, she might mention it to those I would not willingly offend."

"Odd's faith!" responded the jester, "gratitude to Master Augustus will guarantee her discreetness. Yet may my bauble knock down the brains of my wit, a scant commodity, if I can think how our dear nestling will comport her in this surprisal of illustrious guests."

"But I cannot imagine that the successor of Dame Vintry has been heedless of the apt refinements meet for Lady Louise's estate."

"Gentle blood being the native stream of Lady Louise's veins," returned Littlewit, "the refining process was not so difficult as some had forebode. No, beshrew their malice! it came genially, like the polishing touch of goldsmith's work upon the pure ore; and Louise of Alba wears not one mark assorted with base metal."

"This is joy to me," responded Augustus; "I would you could give me assurance that Lady Louise has been also enriched by time with some personal advantages."

" I may prove myself but a partial witness," said Littlewit, " yet do I think, Master Fitzwalter, that not a sweeter face will be amongst you. I declare that the admiration of our earl may now be taken by the nose. That leading feature, though not apt in progress for rising in the world, has at length formed its altitude in high beauty on the face of Lady Louise."

Augustus expressed his surprise and pleasure; and then proceeded to state his wishes that Lady Louise's toilette should be made with care, to receive the coming guests; while as to the castle, he said, he cared not how comfortless they might find it: this important conference ended, Augustus galloped away to join the party on its progress, and Littlewit hastened home to perform his mission.

It is now time to mention, that shortly after Lord Harcourt's peremptory mandate for the dismissal of Dame Vintry had reached Alba Castle, a new lord abbot was appointed to the supremacy of the monastery of St. Stephen's, lately become vacant; and to the utter amazement of Father Jonathan, this new lord abbot presented him with advantageous church preferment; and being, as lord abbot of St. Stephen's, one of the trustees appointed by the late Lord Harcourt for the care of Lady Adela's younger children's portions, took upon himself, as such trustee, to request permission of Lord Harcourt to act a tutelary guardian's part by his fair young neighbour Lady Louise, and as such to recommend a successor for Father Jonathan; a request to which the delighted parent most gratefully acceded; and scarcely had the venerable Father Adrian made his appearance in Alba Castle as preceptor to Lady Louise, when a successor for Dame Vintry was procured also by the active lord abbot, and not objected to by the abbess of St. Mildred's; and this new governess—an ex-recluse from one of the lately dissolved monasteries—Sister Bella, now styled Mrs. Morton, was so completely every thing that could be wished for in the department she now filled, that Littlewit would have immediately given the intelligence received from Augustus to Mrs. Morton, for her to use her own discretion relative to Lady Louise, only that he felt he could not withhold the name of the herald from Mrs. Morton; therefore, in faith to Fitzwalter, he despatched his communications by Maud to Lady Louise.

These communications were heard with surprise, but not with pleasure, by Lady Louise, who with glowing cheeks vehemently exclaimed, " Nothing shall lead my comportment to be, for the king's comfort, beseeming a right loyal subject. If his majesty chooses to come hither without notice, he must be content with damp ungarnished chambers. Ay, in sooth, neither to Master Fitzwalter nor his advice will I yield attention; for I will not apparel myself with any care, nor be loyal in any respect. No; were I to peril my life by it, I would not damage my gratitude to poor Queen Anne by paying homage to her assassin. And were Master Augustus also, to get cold, I will not pity him, since he thus cowers as courtier to the sanguinary Henry. And yet I think, my Maudy," continued Louise, as a sudden thrill of more kindly emotion began to melt the vehemence of her childish petulance, " that would be cruel, not to feel pity for Master Augustus; and a crime too, to yield him no assistance; for he took pity on my cries, when the flames encompassed my baby brother and myself. Yes, yes, Maudy; it would be ill-natured to show recklessness to Augustus, should illness betide him through the damps of our unaired chambers:" and pearly drops now came trickling down the cheeks of Louise, called forth by gratitude, and increased by penitence for the cruelty she had meditated; but very soon her tears were arrested by a new apprehension which struck her active fancy—that were the king not received with every demonstration of loyal respect, he might avenge it upon Augustus as being 'squire to the lord of Alba Castle; as Henry was not one to hear the plea of justice in his court of conscience. And should he discover," continued Louise, "that Augustus gave advice of his repair to Alba, he might lay the blame of his scant and shabby reception upon poor Augustus. Certes," at length Louise exclaimed, "it is my bounden duty to feel loyal. My sovereign not making good view of his duties is no excuse for any lack in mine. No, my Maudy, that would not plead in my behoof at the bar of bars. So I must receive this pitiless king with meet comportment, as if he were the goodly Alfred himself, or the dear Black Prince. But Maud," continued Louise, dimpled smiles making playful efforts to become more visible around her mouth, " do you think hair ever really stands uprightly through influence of fright? If so, as mine has extended in growth, and now is a good length, albeit my honoured father had once thought I was doomed to a bald pate, like an ugly dwarf he had seen at Rome, it may arise to bewray me when I behold this king of terrors. Must I shave my head to keep it on? or think you we can muster enough of array of bodkins to bind over this said witness from appearing against my loyalty?"

This burst of natural vivacity was succeeded by thoughtfulness upon the possibilities to be attempted in preparing for the coming guests; and wishing to question Littlewit upon all that Fitzwalter said, she had him summoned.

"Are you quite certain, Littlewit," demanded Louise, "that Master Fitzwalter said he cared not how the castle might be trapped?"

"As certain, lady," said Littlewit, " as that, in the bright days which are agone, I should have had my finery and my wit to brush up."

"But in our dark age," responded Louise, smiling, " you must leave your wit and finery to lack their burnishing; or they would outdazzle our unfurnished castle, that cannot raise one foot of arras to bedeck its walls, or a measure of fair tapestry, or a glittering cruise to deck a cupboard with."

"Ah, odd's wail! all swept off the stage of once-shining talents, of silver and of gold," rejoined the jester. " In sooth, our sovereign lord the King will soon hie him hence in contempt of this once-vaunted castle. But bear memory, lady, our young courier expressed his wish, that you should make appearance in so much contrast to the deserted castle as conveniently became you. Yet, heaven forfend, there is no prize to be made of Louise of Alba intended. But no, no; Master Fitzwalter would not in that case have meddled in the matter."

"Nay, Littlewit, your memory is short," exclaimed Louise, " or it would hold in remembrance, that Louise of Alba is not so favoured by fortune as to range her amid prizes meet to covet or bestow."

"If fortune do not form the Lady Louise's garnish," said the jester, "there are nobles in her heart's coffer meet for domestic consolation, more *ennobling* than her birth, and of more advantage than fortune ever enriched with. But rumour has whispered in the ear of folly—and fools and children are vehicles for truth—that our late honoured lord took especial care for the content of Lady Adela's

younger race. And rumour may have reached the hearing of court-folk, as aptly as of other long-eared animals; and through this information they repair hither, to see if Lady Louise's manors (manners) are attractive, her hyde (hide) fair, and her fyfe (fife) accomplishments in harmony with their wishes."

"Hold, good jester," said Louise; "and do not imagine the approach of phantoms when substantial matters have taken unpleasant forms for our perplexity; and none of which grieve me like my sad breach in promise of the dole."

Littlewit now ventured to announce to Louise, that Master Fitz-walter, knowing that she could not, without betraying to the steward the intimation he had secretly given of the coming guests, demand a supply for largesse to heralds and other causes, had done himself the honour of leaving in her father's place a purse to answer present exigencies.

With gratitude Lady Louise accepted Augustus's kind loan; and as they were not to expect the coming guests ere noontide, she set out immediately, under the protection of Maud and Littlewit, to restore peace and comfort to a distressed neighbour; and then to wend her way to the hermitage of St. Stephen's valley, to request the venerable recluse who inhabited the lonely dwelling not to visit the castle at present. To the utter marvel of Lady Louise, she found the recluse in full possission of the information which, in faith to Augustus, she had not even imparted to Mrs. Morton or Father Adrian. How the hermit in his lonely dell had acquired intelligence of a party being in progress for Alba, and that Fitzwalter had conveyed secret intimation of it to her, she feared to ask him; but his knowledge of the matter afforded her great comfort; since she felt assured he would not betray Augustus, and she had now an adviser open to her upon whose counsel she could rely.

Louise, feeling that her absence from the castle must be brief, else she could not comply with the request of Augustus relative to her own appearance, could only tarry to obtain a very few words of advice; and, with a heart glowing with gratitude to this venerable recluse, she arose from the moss-clad bench on which she had rested, to take her departure: the hermit also arose; and, to the surprise of Louise, took up his staff and set out with her.

"I will walk through the valley with you," said he; "your attendants will keep at a respectful distance; therefore, without dread of their babbling, I may venture to speak upon the concern of the amiable Fitzwalter. Louise, learn, that through the discontent of the youth upon the method in which you were brought up, the friends and foes of his house were led to exertions in your behalf. Through his view of the matter, I, who had only just entered yon dwelling, was led to yield to you the knowledge which I acquired in a life of travel, study, and experience. From much opportunity thus yielded me of developing your character, I feel perfect assurance in trusting you. Causes prevent my yet seeking Augustus Fitzwalter; it could serve for nothing, and I forbear to encounter him with the cruelty of uncertainty. But you tell him, my child, when none is near to hear the matter, he has a friend whom yet knows not; whose heart is with him; one who will not rest, until he wrests his fortune from the foemen of his illustrious house:—and give heed my dear child, when you tell him this, it must be with the lack of all clue for guidance to me individually."

The astonished Lady Louise attempted to give utterance to some of those powerful feelings which these communications had awakened; but excess of gratitude for all the benefits which she had received from this recluse, with those he thus promised for Augustus, destroyed her eloquence; however, the hermit was satisfied; and kindly turned the conversation to a question which she had asked ere they had left the hermitage, and had not yet been answered:—" Whether the conceal- ment necessary for the continuance of her progress in knowledge, which was thought advisable for her adoption, were to be extended to Fitzwalter ?"

" There is no need for my saying to the daughter of the peerles[s] Adela," he now replied, " to make no unmeet exhibition of her acquisi- tions, even to her truest friends. But, my child, ever[y] throw off disguise with Fitzwalter, when none are near for observance, whom it is convenient not to undeceive in their credence of your mind having remained as unfurnished as had been imagined for you by your foes. But we have arrived at the point where we must part. Farewell !— May heaven's blessings go with you, my child !"

Lady Mary now parted from this venerable and mysterious friend, full of gratitude for herself and Augustus; yet not untinctured with some uneasy fears of preternatural influence. The knowlege of Au- gustus's interview with Littlewit, and its purport, having reached the hermitage of St. Stephen's valley as if borne thither on the wings of magic, restored some apprehensions to her bosom of the recluse, its present inhabitant, being versed in necromancy; for she had sometimes fancied the ever closely hooded hermit could put on or off old age at pleasure: since, at times, her eye had detected the soft and gentle falter of decreasing vocal energy, in her friend of the valley, changed to the less natural tones of a more powerful voice, creaking its efforts to imitate senescence; she had marked the graceful bending of declining strength transformed to the sharper curving of one who could stand erect; and she watched for some proof to attest these transmutations into comparative youth, that she might impart her surmises to Maud, but in vain; for only when the form and voice of age were unequivocal, were his instructions for Louise's improvement yielded. Although in both forms, she marked, he had appeared to, and conversed with, not only Maud, Mrs. Morton, and Father Adrian, but with the lord abbot of St. Stephen's himself; yet none of them had seemed aware of the changes she perceived, and which she acknowledged to herself were cer- tainly scarcely perceptible.

CHAPTER XV.

THE rays of the sun announced to Louise and attendants that they had no time to lose in regaining home, to make their toilette for the recep- tion of the expected guests; their speed homeward was, therefore, fleet from the moment they parted with the recluse; yet, had they only en- tered the court of the castle, when the sudden sound of trumpets, and of the trampling of horses upon the draw-bridge, which had not been raised since lowered for the egress of Lady Louise, proclaimed to them and to the amazed porter, the approach of something like a multitude. The voice of a *pursuivant* now, with pompous gravity, demanded entrance for his sovereign lord the king, consort, and suite, into the Castle of Alba.

Louise, trembling like an aspen branch, faltered out the order for admission, which the porter with tremulous hands obeyed, and Lady Louise, almost intuitively, advanced, with lingering steps and bounding heart, to perform her painful task of giving welcome to the sovereign from whom gratitude to the memory of Anne Boleyn bid her recoil; and poor Louise was destined thus to make, in this presentation of herself, an exhibition that yielded pastime for the frolickers, such as they expected.

Although to Henry the Eighth we are indebted for the first institution of the comfortable system which enables us to travel with speed and convenience, yet the bye-ways, in 1536, which pedestrians had to wade through, had not yet come under the royal consideration, and bore no similitude to those in our days of improvement. The hose and kirtle, therefore, of Lady Louise, bore conspicuous testimony of how much wet had fallen in the night; and her garb was anything but such as Louise should ever have been doomed to wear; but her apparel was furnished by the abbess of St. Mildred's; and, through the influence of Isabel, was ever calculated to impede the acquirement of any taste in the fancy or arrangement of her attire.

Such was the state of Louise's dress at this critical moment; but to describe her personal appearance is a task no less difficult than mortifying; the traces of the copious floods of tears which she had that morning shed upon the discovery that her means of charity had vanished, were still visible on all her features; the varied sensations which had agitated her mind since the first intelligence conveyed from Augustus to the present moment, with her rapid flight from St. Stephen's valley, had beamed their accumulating flushes over her countenance to a disfiguring degree; and alarm, and other painful sensations, lent their potent aid to take from her appearance every symptom of composure; overpowered by all that was opening before her, she stood perfectly amazed.

With the *pursuivant* and heralds, first came prancing into the court a group of the pretended lords and ladies attendant upon their Majesties; amongst whom were the laughter-loving Sir Lionel, and the portentous Sir Rupert. Next in the gorgeous cavalcade came pacing in, on beautiful white palfreys, gaily trapped, the representatives of the king and queen; then followed the fair and smiling Blanch Worlington and Augustus Fitzwalter; after whom, came rumbling over the hollow-sounding drawbridge, the first of the showily garnished pleasure waggons. But the scared spirit of poor Louise waited not to behold more of the imposing pageant; for heralds, and 'squires, and knights, and ladies, and queens, and kings, she had never seen before except in pictures: the embodying such spectacles, and under such circumstances, proved too mighty for the volatile Louise, who achieved but one actual glance at the entering groups, and the next moment found her extended at the feet of Maud in total insensibility.

The anxious Augustus, who had taken in at one penetrating glance the whole unprepossessing appearance which Lady Louise had thus exhibited, was full of bitter disappointment relative to this object of his long fraternal interest; and, not a little mortified at her so obviously paying no attention to his earnest request relative to her toilette, he was not sufficiently active to prove the first by offering kindly assistance. Sir Rupert Fitzstephen, therefore, was the first to vault from his steed, to raise up the swooning lady of the castle from the arms of Maud; and to bear her triumphantly into the hall, where, on an oaken table, she was placed by him with a show of tenderness becoming a knight or courteous gentleman: and no man present, not even Sir Lionel himself, considered that tenderness misapplied, when they looked upon her graceful form.

The trumpets of the pretended heralds had attracted every inhabitant of the castle, with all convenient speed, to learn the cause of the sounding of a clarion within the castle of forsaken Alba—some in terror, some through curiosity, but all in *deshabille*—for seclusion with inaction, and a total absence of all stimulus to emulation or exertion, had engendered sloth and carelessness to appearance in the household and retainers in this once populous and magnificent castle. In strange diversity of apparel, therefore—some completing their toilette as they rushed onward—this general muster appeared; and this strange gathering had but just commenced their assembling in the base court, when Lady Louise fainted; but soon the reiterated cry that she was dead led all from the scene so gratifying to their own curiosity to relieve their alarms and anxiety relative to Louise, by following Sir Rupert into the hall.

The general grief of the household, and evident interest of many amongst the new arrivals, for the swooning Louise, struck with discord upon the observation of the invidious Isabel, who, shrinking from recognition, had entered the castle closely veiled; and, with increased discord in her feelings, she with dismay beheld, in the inanimate face and form before her, destruction to almost every hope and expectation her enmity had cherished; whilst, in that very inanimation, a guarantee for sensibility appeared, that might, on other occasions as well as the present, excite an interest which she had predetermined the hated Louise should never awaken: for now she beheld, whilst standing in ambush to detect their treasons, even the seneschal, whose devotedness to her cause she had been fully assured of, and the traitor Father Nicoli, evincing sympathy; particularly the former, who flew about to procure restoratives, as if his own life were depending upon the recovery of Lady Louise. To terminate these annoyances for the present, and to impede the progress of interest for the noxious Louise, Isabel hastened to instruct the pretended queen to issue her royal mandate, in the soft and alluring semblance of humanity, to have the poor suffering invalid conveyed to her own chamber—a mandate which was accordingly obeyed.

This removal of Lady Louise from public view allowed the thoughts of all the inhabitants of the castle, who did not accompany the beloved object of their interest to her chamber, to turn upon the late arrivals; and, finding it seriously pronounced to be the royal party on a progress, the consternation awakened became highly relished amusement for those who caused it; for whose accommodation every possible arrangement was instantly commenced; yet, save in the instance of removing the glass windows from their depositories to a reinstatement in the frames they were formed to occupy, all was pitiable, nay, pitiful, deficiency.

At length the aspect of all things changed, by the arrival of carts bearing the household stuff from Vespasian tower, and which now were introduced as pertaining to the court; but, strange to the perplexed household, whose memory Isabel had failed to calculate upon, almost every individual of them had before seen some old acquaintance, which seemed to find its ready fitment, as if in an ancient resting place: and while the nailing up of tapestry and arras on the walls—spreading them out on cupboards—laying down patches of curious carpets amid newly strewn rushes—resting cushions on long beraved chairs and window-seats—hoisting canopies over bedsteads and seats of estate—scarcely one hand now worked in this animating employment who did not detect some article, in this supply from the royal stores, to awaken suspicion that the providers must be dealers, at least, in necromancy, if not in other sleight of hand, so marvellously had they suited their suppletory cargo to the various ranges of apartments and offices upon the premises. And most of the comparatively few individuals now in Alba Castle to fill up these once regally supplied departments, at length ventured to murmur conjectures to each other upon the appalling possibility of some dire magic being once more in operation over the house of Harcourt; and, upon those who were thus superstitiously alarmed, fear of individual consequences proved an excellent spur to industry for the accommodation of the powerful fiends who worked these spells.

But whilst all this alarm of magic and light fingers, and this revival of long dormant industry, were operating through the household, the thoughts of Isabel found full employment too. The long eye-lashes, the finely formed eye-brows, nose, and mouth, which the face of Lady Louise had exhibited as she lay inanimate, filled her stepdame with surprise how a child could have so completely changed its mould in growing towards maturity; and with dismay, because in this transformation she portrayed a striking resemblance to her father. How, therefore, could she (Isabel) ever attempt to lead the general voice against the beauty of his daughter, without offending the personally vain Lord Harcourt. The household, she had found reason to believe, were all devoted to this object of her long-cherished enmity: and how to take any effective measures to counteract this partiality, whilst under her assumed character, she could not devise; and, miserable in this state of suspended malace, she determined to betray her identity to Father Nicoli, with whom she soon effected a private conference.

To her amazed auditor, Lady Harcourt acknowledged the deception of personages who had entered the castle with her; commanding, at the same time, the preservation of the secret until she should grant permission to disclose it; and this confession made she gave full scope to her irritated feelings, by demanding, indignantly, " Why he had evinced so much anxiety about Lady Louise ?"

The tone in which this query was delivered, informed the wily Nicoli how he must reply ; and, waiving the fact of what had actually operated upon him until he should receive instructions from the abbess of St. Mildred's, he, with plausible craft, replied :—" That being known by all the household as devoted to her interest, he had conceived it sound policy, for her sake, to assume the aspect of strong interest for her step-child ; and to impress his majesty and courtiers, by whom he had believed himself surrounded, with the conviction that this seeming kindliness beamed through his bosom as the mere reflection from that of his influential sun—his generous and kind-hearted patroness and honoured lady."

This wily fabrication fully satisfied Isabel of his fealty; yet she remained doubtful whether to admit the solidity of the policy in its effect.

" But," she peevishly exclaimed, " is it also for my satisfaction that Davenant, by taking the same view of the matter, has assumed the semblance of interest in Lady Louise ? If his was mumming, it marvellously took the guise, I think, of breach of faith."

Davenant, the seneschal, was at this time at open warfare with Father Nicoli, upon a recent occurrence in the castle ; the holy father, therefore, felt it wholly unnecessary to make the peace of Master Seneschal with the indignant countess. He consequently answered drily, that he was not in Davenant's secrets.

" I intend instantly to discover if his anxiety was also hypocritical," said the alarmed Isabel. " Send for him hither, and under the shadow of my hood, and in this corner I can sit in ambush, while you question him if he stands faithful to me ?"

The seneschal was accordingly summoned, and Nicoli, in consequence of their hostility, yielded no intimation of how the former might commit himself by replying ingenuously to the abrupt question— " How he came to show so much interest for Lady Louise, and seem so despairing when she was in her swoon ?"

" What is that to thee, most holy sire ?" returned the seneschal, contemptuously, casting his penetrating eyes in bitter scorn upon his interrogator. " It seems to me it would be more for the honour of thy cloth to appoint thyself to the composing of moralities to deck the strong boxes of the new-come guests. Such like as ' Honesty is the best policy.' "

Father Nicoli, although visibly disconcerted, made no comment upon this rude retort; but, with more mildness, repeated his question.

" By whose command am I cited to the question ?" demanded the seneschal, haughtily. " Beshrew me, if I answer thee, until I know the mover of this daring."

" The mandate for this question came from sovereign authority," responded Father Nicoli, mildly.

" If from the holy office itself," returned the seneschal, " I have only one reply for my averment—Through gratitude."

" Traitor ! base and recreant !" exclaimed the agitated Isabel, led, by her frantic indignation, out of self-possession. " Does the mark of gratitude to Louise of Alba accord with what you owed to him whom the cruelty of this very Louise's mother consigned to misery?"

" Lady," replied the startled Davenant, resuming quickly his composure, " I am no traitor; although gratitude to Lady Louise has found a place in my breast. Three years since, repairing to the castle battlements to see to some matters that were in jeopardy, I fell through an embrasure, and dislocated an arm and fractured a leg. I was alone, and fainted. On recovery, I found my head supported by the gentle child; she whom, for two long years, I had treated with every species of unkindness that could annoy her; nay, in my cruelty, with more than unkindly treatment. Yes; Louise of Alba, lady, heard my groans, and winged her way to find out who was there so hurt; and there, to her surprise, she found the surly, savage seneschal in extreme need, and in that moment her heart expunged all record of my ill-nature. Revenge is not in Lady Louise's heart—but Christian kindness and charity. She brought me aid, and devised for my comfort and consolation all that would assist in my recovery; and to her I owe it. This Lady Louise I found frightened into a swoon. I am no monster of ingratitude; and aid and sympathy it were but meet in me to pay to my preserver."

The agitated seneschal now wiped away the tears of gratitude which had started to his eyes; and, with a more steady voice, continued— " I waited not one moment needlessly, ere I informed the lady abbess of St. Mildred's, that no feeling of vengeance for the cruelty of Lady Adela to my beloved master should in future actuate me. The lady of St. Mildred's reply was, that I had only spoken the Countess of Harcourt's intention; for that the wish of that lady was the prosperity of Lady Louise. If the holy mother spoke falsely, the fault is not mine. My motive is now without disguise before my honoured lady; that purpose can never be vanquished. I will now retire, and in respectfulness await the decision, as to my fitness, or otherwise, of retaining my present station."

Davenant now made his obeisance and retired, leaving the disconcerted Isabel convinced that her friend's policy was good, in affirming a change in plans and wishes to one who had unequivocally confessed a variation in his own; and under the influence of this policy she would have instantly acted, had she not been too much unhinged by this unexpected desertion of the seneschal, to accomplish it with her usual deceitful management; whilst as to Father Nicoli, he was not that acquired villian she imagined him to be, and became convinced ere too late of her fatal errors. She therefore resolved to turn repentant of her sins, and make every reparation in her power, to the lovely Lady Louise and her Father. And retire into a Convent, to end her days, in prayers, and self mortifications; trusting thereby to make her peace with the offended Almighty, and those beings, she so cruelly injured upon earth.

THE END.